NOTHING LASTS FOREVER

RODERICK THORP

BALLANTINE BOOKS • NEW YORK

Library of Congress Catalog Card Number: 79-15366

ISBN 0-345-28781-9

This edition published by arrangement with W. W. Norton
& Company

Manufactured in the United States of America

First Ballantine Books Edition: July 1983

December 24

"WHAT I DON'T understand," the taxi driver shouted over the whacking of the windshield wipers, "is what goes through a person's mind when he mutilates somebody like that."

As he glanced over his shoulder in conversational emphasis, the white station wagon thirty feet in front suddenly braked, skidding in the accumulating slush, its massive back end rising like a sounding whale. The passenger in the taxi, Joseph Leland, who had been wondering about something else entirely, perplexed, threw up his hands; the driver reacted, banging his foot on the brake pedal and twisting the wheel. The taxi pitched forward, rotating slowly on its vertical axis, and slammed sideways into the wagon. The right side of Leland's forehead struck the doorpost, drawing blood. He braced for another collision with the car behind, but none came.

"Shit!" the driver cried, punching the steering wheel. "Shit!"

"Are you all right?" Leland asked.

"Yeah." He saw Leland. "Ah, damn. Damn!"

"Don't worry about it." On Leland's handkerchief was a jagged stain of blood the size of a postage stamp.

The driver was black, young, with high cheekbones and almond eyes. He and Leland had been discussing atrocities in Africa. The falling snow had made the ride from the hotel near the huge, stainless steel Gateway downtown a long one; Leland had learned that the driver had come to St. Louis from Birmingham as a single man in the late fifties, and that his son was now an all-city third baseman for his high school team.

In the bumper-to-bumper traffic near the airport, the conversation turned to violence. As he wheeled the taxi from the Interstate to the airport approach road, the driver brought up the recent sexual maimings in black Africa. *Lambert* Field, Leland realized, with the driver talking about severed penises. Not Lindbergh, in spite of the St. Louis connection. Lindbergh, a dangerous airport, was in San Diego. Leland had been in and out of St. Louis a dozen times in the past five years, and this was not the first time he had made the mistake.

Now he was bleeding: for a lot of people, a mature man with a cut on his brow was a falling-down drunk. In spite of that unnerving prospect, Leland was neither upset nor angry. It was not really a bad cut. Because of the accident, he had lost track of something else that had crossed his mind. It began to nag at him. He worked up a new blot on the handkerchief.

"I'm sorry, man. I'm really sorry."

Leland could see it. Now the driver of the wagon opened his door and looked back, unwilling to step out into the mess on the roadway. He was a big, fat man with a moustache, a man-mountain, the kind cops were always careful with. He had a temper to match, too: he scowled at the taxi driver, and jerked his thumb commandingly in the direction of the shoulder of the road. The station wagon rolled forward, spewing slush up against Leland's side of the car.

"My plane is leaving in twenty minutes," Leland said.

"Right. That guy can see me down at the terminal. I'm sorry, man. I really am sorry." He stopped beside the station wagon, reached over and lowered the right front window, allowing the whirling snow to funnel inside.

"Pull over!" the big man bellowed.

"My passenger's bleeding and has to catch a plane—"

"Don't give me that crap! Pull over!"

Leland cranked down the rear window. "Let me get to the terminal."

The big man studied him a moment. "You're not hurt that bad. Do you know what this guy is going to try on me? Pull over!" he shouted to the taxi driver.

"He has to catch a plane!"

4

"Don't fuck with me, you goddamned nigger! As soon as he's out of the cab, you'll take off!"

The taxi driver stepped on the gas. "Fuck yourself!" he shouted. He nearly lost control of the vehicle again as he struggled to close the window. "I don't have to put up with that shit!"

"He's a psycho," Leland said. "Here's my card. I'll be in California for the next ten days, then I'll be back east. Later, if he makes trouble for you, I'll give you any kind of deposition you want."

"It's not later I'm worried about," the driver said. "I'm worried about now."

"As long as I'm in the cab," Leland said, "we have an ace in the hole."

The driver glanced in the mirror. "He got back in the traffic. You some kind of a cop?"

"More of a consultant, these days." Leland patted his forehead again. "The important thing is that I'm carrying the iron that makes it official."

"Jesus. You never do know, do you? Hey, here's something I always wanted to know: How do you get that thing on the plane?"

"They issue a card. Very special. It can't be copied."

"Sure, right, they would have a card. That's funny, like the commercials. Do you know me?" he mocked. He made a gun of his hand. "This is the *real* American Express."

Leland grinned. "I'll have to remember that."

The bleeding had lessened, but now his head throbbed. It was going to get worse. The traffic slowed, and the driver glanced up and then over to the mirror on the door.

"Here he comes."

The wagon was on their left. The big man swung it over so that it skidded against the taxicab. Leland moved over and lowered the side window.

"Don't plug him, man, please."

"These guys plug themselves," Leland said, enjoying the old slang. Like so many blacks, the driver had the gift of language—he had wanted to know what went through a *person's* mind. Leland had wondered about the driver's choice of words in that context—and then he remembered

5

something else, the thing that had begun eluding him with the accident. "I'm a police officer," Leland shouted to the big man. "Let us get to the terminal!"

"I told him not to fuck with me! Now I'm telling you the same!" the big man roared, and turned his steering wheel so that the wagon continued to press against the taxi. Leland was thinking of a guy like this who had held off a dozen policemen in a bowling alley in New Jersey, heaving bowling balls like cantaloupes. There was no telling how wild this one was. Leland drew his Browning 9 millimeter, made sure the safety was on, and pushed it through the open windows toward the big man's nose. The Browning was a professional's handgun, thirteen shots in the magazine and room for one in the clip, which was empty now. The big man saw Leland's seriousness. His eyes rolled back and his tongue protruded, curled like a canapé. He thought Leland was going to shoot him in the face . . . to get on a plane.

"He'll see you at the terminal," Leland said to him.

The big man was motionless, afraid to move. The taxi driver eased forward, the fenders scraping.

"Jesus," the driver said.

Leland was trembling, nearly sick. He could be in deep trouble—at least, have some serious explaining in store. "I made a mistake," he said to the driver quickly. "It's just a fender-bender. If he tries to push you around, we'll both charge him with assault."

"Hey, man, don't worry about it. I saw no gun."

Leland got twenty-five dollars out of his wallet. The curving ramp up to the terminal emerged from the falling snow.

"California, huh?" the driver asked. "I've never had the pleasure."

"I'm going to see my daughter in Los Angeles. Then I'm going to drive up the coast to Eureka to see an old friend."

"Your daughter married?"

"Divorced. She has two children. Her mother's dead, but we were divorced, too, years ago."

"Well, you'll be with your family," the driver said. "That's the important thing. Me, too. I'm going to have a good Christmas in spite of this. I'll tell you, man, I've never had much luck with Christmas. When I was a little boy, my

6

daddy used to get drunk and beat up on me. I guess it's not all clear sailing for anybody—"

A 747 rose up over the roof of the terminal, blackening the fishbelly sky and drowning the driver's last words. The station wagon glided by again, the big man glowering at them warily. Leland got another ten from his wallet, then, almost as an after-thought, the I.D. that would get the Browning, loaded, onto the airplane. While the gun was legal, a badge he was carrying was not. It was a New York City detective's badge, a gift from friends in that department, the back engraved THIS MAN IS A PRICK. Leland pushed the twenty-five over the front seat.

The driver pulled to the curb and flipped the meter flag. "Oh, no, man, this is on me."

"Merry Christmas," Leland said, thrusting the money at him. "Have a nice holiday."

The driver took it. The station wagon pulled in front of the taxi. A skycap opened Leland's door. As he got out, Leland gave him the ten. "Get a cop, pronto. The luggage goes to Los Angeles."

"Yes, sir. I'll get somebody to ticket your bags. You have yourself a Merry Christmas."

Leland felt the beginning of relief. This morning's "Good Morning, America" had reported Los Angeles at seventy-eight degrees. A cop was coming through the terminal crowd toward the automatic doors. Leland raised his hand to hold the cop inside. "Stay in your seat," he called to the driver. "Merry Christmas to you."

"You, too. Thanks for your help. Have a nice flight."

Leland felt he was abandoning the man. Inside the terminal, he produced for the cop, another black man, the I.D. Woven into the plastic of the card was a coded array of rare metals, and now they sparkled under the terminal lights.

"Oh, yeah, right, I know you." The cop, whose name was JOHNSON, T.E., looked over Leland's shoulder, "What's the problem?"

Leland explained that he had been in the taxi during the accident and that the driver of the wagon had gone berserk.

Patrolman Johnson eyed Leland. "You wave your piece at him?"

"I told him I had it," Leland lied.

7

He smiled and glanced at the taxi. "Sounds good. The brother with you on this? Don't juice my fruit."

Leland grinned. "Scout's honor. I'd salute, but I'd start bleeding again."

"You better have that looked at. Go ahead. Don't worry about this. Have a nice holiday."

"Same to you." Leland kept the identification in hand for the officer at the metal detector. He blotted his forehead again—now he had four large stains on the handkerchief. He had a look at himself in a mirror in the window of a gift shop. It was a real cut, all right, but not deep and barely half an inch long. Something was still bothering him. The officer at the metal detector was another black man: LOPEZ, R.A. Spanish father and black mother? The combination was more common in Los Angeles, and for a second it made Leland wonder dizzily if he had stepped through the looking glass.

"What flight are you taking?"

"The 905, as far as Los Angeles. I'll be in first class, a Christmas present to myself."

"Well, that'll be a helluva flight for somebody to try to hijack. There's two shore patrol riding in economy through to San Diego, and a federal marshal up front with you. I'll let you figure out who he is."

"More important, you'd better let him know who *I* am."

Officer Lopez laughed silently. "I'm going to call ahead. What did you do, slip on the ice?"

"Fender-bender. Nothing serious."

"Well, have a nice flight. See how long it takes you to figure out who the marshal is."

"Thanks, I love puzzles."

The clock in the check-in lounge read 4:04, and passengers were still filing into the umbilical ramp. Leland asked the clerk if he had time for a long-distance call.

"Oh, you'll be sitting here for quite a few minutes, sir. They're backed up half an hour trying to get equipment out of St. Louis. This is a bad one. We'll shut down by eight o'clock."

"There's no chance of us not getting out, is there?"

"No," the clerk said, as if Leland were being foolish.

It took the operator a moment to record Leland's credit

card number and put the call through, and another before his daughter's secretary picked up the extension.

"Oh, Mr. Leland, she's still out to lunch. You're going to be on the same flight, aren't you?"

He had forgotten the time differential.

"Yes, but I think it's going to be a little late. There's a blizzard here. That's not what I called about." He didn't know if he should continue. "I was in a little accident outside the airport. I'm not hurt, but I do have a cut on my forehead—"

"Oh, you poor man. How do you feel?"

"Well, I guess a little shaken, but I'm all right. I didn't want Stephanie—Ms. Gennaro—getting upset when she saw me."

"I'll tell her. Don't worry about a thing."

There was a tapping on the telephone booth door: a flight attendant, a woman of thirty-five, her dyed bright yellow hair rolled in a style that dated back to the Kennedy years. KATHI LOGAN, according to her nameplate. Now that she had his attention, she smiled brightly, too youthfully, and did a little curtsying nod. Leland said good-bye to the secretary, being careful not to hang up while she too was wishing him a good flight, and opened the door. Kathi Logan spoke with a professional cheer.

"Mr. Leland? Are you ready now? We've all been waiting for you."

The plane was forty-five minutes getting to the runway. He had to stay in his seat, but Kathi Logan brought him some moistened and dry tissues, her mirror, a Band-Aid, and finally, two aspirin tablets. After she had elicited from him that he was going to visit his daughter, a subtle warmth began to creep into her behavior, indicating she was not a bad detective herself. He was wearing no rings, and a man didn't travel to see his daughter at Christmas without his wife, if he had one. But that was a long way from knowing who he was, or even if he had told the truth about himself. Obviously she was alone, felt she was getting older, and a little frightened. He knew the feeling, and that she still spelled her name cute only made him like her more.

9

The plane was filled, more like a suburban commuter train than a flight across half a continent. The fellow sitting next to the window had his face in a magazine. Not the federal marshal, he was too small to pass the physical. In her effort to help, Kathi Logan had said that the storm extended to the western edge of Iowa, making the first hour of the flight rocky, so she wouldn't be able to let Leland out of his seat to clean up in the washroom. Leland's seatmate had overheard, and Leland saw him tighten his grip on his *Newsweek*.

From the war on, Leland had flown his own planes for more than twenty years, working his way up to a Cessna 310 before he quit. Now he paid no more attention to aviation than any other constant passenger, but he knew that this latest generation of aircraft was the safest ever built. The real problem these days was human error.

And as for the possibility of air piracy, although none had occurred in the United States in years, there was enough good-guy ordnance aboard to butcher all the people in the no-smoking section. Leland wondered if the marshal on board knew that the other armed passenger in first class had helped design the program that had created his job. At the height of the piracy, Leland had been consulted by the FAA, and now he was caught in the situation the program had been designed to prevent: too many guns. Years had passed since he had had contact with any of it, and because he did not know the latest revisions in procedure, Leland was as good as not trained at all, like the S.P.'s in economy. Too many guns and not enough training. If he was on edge, it was because he knew too much.

The plane was next in line. A porpoise-nosed DC-10 slipped by in the darkness, followed by the muffled roar of its engines. The 747 started rolling again, and Kathi Logan appeared at his side, steadying herself against the rocking of the aircraft.

"How about a drink before we get in the air? Would you like a double scotch?"

He smiled. "You wouldn't like me any more. Can I have a Coke? I could use the sugar."

"Sure."

The pilot was turning for the takeoff run when Kathi Logan came back with the Coke on a tray. She had another smile for him, then hurried back to her seat next to the spiral staircase to the upper deck. Apparently the notion that he was a drunk trying to stay retired did not frighten her. The pilot pushed the throttles to full power. Halfway down the runway, the nose lifted like the end of a teeterboard. Then the rear wheels floated off the ground and they were airborne.

Leland had been sorting out the Lambert-Lindbergh confusion when the driver had asked his amazing question, turning Leland's thoughts completely around. He had been about to tell the driver that he didn't know what went through a person's mind—when he realized suddenly that in fact he did know.

As a young detective years ago he had been on a case in which the victim's penis had been cut off. Leland had followed the chain of evidence along the line of least resistance, to the victim's roommate, a drifter with a criminal record.

After hours of questioning, the drifter, Tesla, finally broke down and confessed. This was in the days when people went to the electric chair every week. Tesla was sentenced to death and electrocuted within the year.

The case brought Leland to public attention for the third time in his life. A rookie patrolman before the war, he had been in a gunfight in which three men had died, including Leland's partner. As a fighter pilot in Europe, he had shot down over twenty Nazi planes, enough to make a New York publisher ask him to write a book. Leland's presence on the Tesla case, with its elements of forbidden sex and lurid mutilations, made it a media event years before such things had labels. When Leland's personal life shattered not long afterward, he was as confused as anyone.

Six years later, when Leland, then running a private detective agency, was asked by a pregnant young woman to investigate her husband's leap or fall from the roof of a racetrack, the evidence led back through Leland's own life to the Tesla case. Leland had sent an innocent man to his grave.

The real killer had been a closet homosexual, unable to accept himself, ravaged with self-hate. His victim, Tesla's roommate, Teddy Leikman, had been a pick-up in a gay bar. At Leikman's apartment, with the hapless Tesla out for the evening, the situation had become more than the killer could bear.

He beat Teddy Leikman to death with his fists, finally crushing his skull with a piece of pottery—but in the struggle, Leikman gouged the other man's neck, getting bits of skin under his fingernails. The solution the killer hit upon came out of the depths of his soul. He severed Leikman's fingers, and to misdirect the police, he severed his penis, too. It worked because no one thought for a moment that the mutilations were anything *but* the act of a man shrieking his hatred of himself.

As an act of self-preservation, the mutilations to conceal evidence finally came to nothing. Six years later, the killer did, indeed, kill himself.

But not before leaving irrefutable evidence of the biggest municipal fraud since the days of Boss Tweed.

It was the killer's widow who suffered most of all. A kid who had come up off the streets, she wanted the truth told— she could see the connection between her late husband's secret torments and the profiteering of his business cohorts. She wanted people to see how such stealing added to the burdens of the poor.

None of that happened. Every one of the conspirators was able to weasel out of going to jail. Instead of focusing on the housing fraud, the newspapers turned to the old case, Leland's war record, and on, and on. When a scandal sheet suggested a romance going on between detective and client, Norma moved to San Francisco. Leland didn't see her again for years.

Leland's Lindbergh—Lambert confusion had its real origins in those years, for he had been that uncomfortable with the personality the media had assigned to him. "Lucky Lindy," he had called himself more than once, in despair. Like the killer who had eluded him, he had been living two lives and lying to himself about what it meant. His marriage had been disintegrating—and of course he had not solved his big case at all, although he did not know that until later.

What went on in a person's mind? Nothing at all—at such times, the mind and body were one. But there, Leland thought, there in the blankness, lay the riddle of history.

THE WEATHER REPORT had been wrong. The cloud cover extended all the way to the Rockies, and now that the sun was below the mountains, the endless billowy carpet had turned to the color of slate. The 747 was at 38,000 feet, and the Rockies looked like a snow-covered archipelago anchored in a fantastic, undiscovered sea.

Leland still loved flying—and happily, he spent more time in the air than ever. He wasn't going to live long enough to get into space, but at times he wondered how close he would be able to come before he died. In the back of his mind was the notion to take a trip to Europe simply to fly over on the *Concorde*. His old wingman Billy Gibbs up in Eureka had not been in an airplane in thirty years. Leland had watched him pull barrel rolls over the English Channel, howling like a savage; but once the war was over, Billy Gibbs put flying out of his mind forever. There was a line in Shakespeare about the fault lying not in our stars, but ourselves. The passage of time had made so much clear. Everything we do, everything that happens to us, rises out of impulses most people can't even feel, much less understand.

After the dinner clamor, he strolled back to the galley to get acquainted with Kathi Logan. After serving a full flight, she looked a little frazzled.

"Thanks for your help."

"Hi. Did the aspirins work?"

"Sure. I'm hoping you do plastic surgery."

She stared at his brow. "No, that isn't elegant."

"How did you spot me back at the airport?"

"You *are* a cop, aren't you? I took the call from the terminal on you. The officer told me you had a cut, but actually I went out there looking for the one who carried a gun. It was a test."

"How did you do?"

"I got an A."

He remembered that a marshal was on the plane. Usually when he was confronted with a problem like that, he had it solved before the plane reached cruise altitude. Under Leland's own rules, Kathi Logan was not supposed to tell him who the guy was.

"Would you like another Coke?"

"Get your work out of the way, first."

"It's no trouble."

"Can I ask what kind of a policeman you are?"

"I'm a consultant on security and police procedures. I just finished a three-day seminar at McDonnell Douglas."

"You make it sound simple. I know how much weight you carry."

He grinned. "My name is Joe."

"I'm Kathi. How long have you been sober?"

He tried to conceal his surprise with her directness. "Oh, a long time. I didn't have a bad case anyway, knocking myself out at night. I quit when I realized I was looking forward to getting loaded at lunch."

"I had to wait until I woke up in Clark County jail. That's Vegas."

"I know."

"Surprised?"

"Not now. In fact, I'm getting to like it."

The plane rocked through another dish-rattling patch of turbulence. She grinned. "You remind me of a boxer I used to know—"

He laughed aloud. "Cut it out."

"No, he was always mannerly and soft-spoken. He never forced himself on people."

"How did he do in the ring?"

"He was welterweight champion of the world."

She kept her eyes on his as he smiled. She was selling hard, but it still felt good. He glanced at the ice in his glass. When he looked up again, she laughed at him silently.

"What I was about to say was that he was shy, too."

*   *   *

15

Kathi Logan had a condo on the beach north of San Diego, a studio with a sleeping loft, fireplace, and skylights. It sounded beautiful. He lived outside of New York in a garden apartment and spent most of his time in Washington and Virginia motel rooms. When he got out to the Coast, it was more of the same in Palo Alto. He had been to Santa Barbara twice. Fortunately, she flew east almost every other week. As long as she was home within seven days to water her plants, her schedule caused her no problems.

He believed it. She was a native Californian, complete with that fierce optimism. She said she would have loved *American Graffiti* if it had been made five years earlier. She had grown up on the beach. "I wasn't exactly an early hippy, but I was sort of semiliberated. I went with it for a long time, up to Vegas for Sinatra's openings, being the champ's girl for a while. It was fun." More turbulence, thumping the bottom of the plane. "I would just as soon forget all the years Nixon was in office. I don't know why, but my whole life just went crappo."

"A cab driver in St. Louis told me Christmas is always hell for him. This right after he ran into a station wagon."

She looked at his Band-Aid. When Stephanie had been a child, he remembered he and Karen had called the Band-Aids for her scrapes "battle ribbons." Kathi Logan could see that he had disappeared inside himself for a moment. "I'm going to visit friends this year," she said. "Tonight I'll get the lights up and watch it on television."

"Have a Merry Christmas, Kathi."

"I will. You have one, too."

The other girl needed drinks for passengers upstairs in the lounge, so Leland stepped out of the way and looked down at the snow blowing off the jagged peaks of the mountains. Human beings could not survive down there, yet here they were floating far above with dinner in their bellies and drinks in their hands, and the loudest sound was that of their conversation.

The geography books of Leland's childhood had made him believe that the Rockies were America's great unconquerable natural wonder. Prices slightly higher west of the Rockies, the ads used to say. Kathi Logan had grown up on

16

the beach. Leland could remember writing to Karen during the war of the world that would come after. In fact, no one could have imagined it. And here he was going with it, as Logan the Californian had just said, playing with the way she expressed herself as much as the cab driver had done back in the snow in St. Louis. In so many ways it was still America the Beautiful, just as it always had been. Robert Frost had explained it in saying we had become the land's—there was a common denominator inside people like the cab driver and Kathi Logan: they were open to themselves, free, and not small, which was the best of the American national identity.

Now you could see the break in the cloud cover, and the desert disappearing into the accumulating purple of twilight.

When Kathi Logan had another break, they started talking again. He told her of his plans to drive up the Coast. Route One, she said; she told him to have lunch on Saturday in Santa Cruz, but she wouldn't tell him why.

They went on. Her idea of a vacation was a week on Kona—more lying on the beach. She kept promising herself that she was going to do some exploring, but she never got around to it. He saw no point in telling her that his "vacations" consisted of those conferences, conventions, and seminars that took him to parts of the world that he didn't need to be reminded of.

Lake Mead, reflecting the sky, and Hoover Dam, a tiny crescent of lights, appeared below. Las Vegas could be seen blinking and flashing to the north. He could tell Logan things about Vegas, but they could wait.

Leland had her telephone number. He was going to call tomorrow night and ask her to meet him in San Francisco. Maybe he was too tame for her. He assumed she knew San Francisco better than he did, and he thought she was the kind of woman who wanted to stay on an even footing with a man. All that was a bore to a kid looking for action, or a forty-year-old recently sprung from a bad marriage, but it was the way he had always been, and he could not function any other way.

The reduction in the power developed by the engines was so gradual that it was on the edge of perception, but the plane was beginning to descend, and the practiced eye could

17

see the desert floor slowly rising, like an oversized elevator.

"I'd better get back to my seat. You have a nice day tomorrow. I think we're going to be friends. We're going to enjoy each other."

She was watching him. "I'd like that, yes."

He touched her arm, an involuntary, unconscious gesture of good-bye, and in the moment he was wondering if he had gone too far, she stepped toward him, surprising herself as he had just been surprised. He kissed her. They were alone. Nobody saw. When they moved away, she was flushed with excitement.

"Mañana," he said, and winked.

She laughed. "Ole!"

He was back in his seat before he thought of the marshal again. The man could know him. What did Leland's behavior look like from that point of view? The idea made Leland uneasy. Under the circumstances, he couldn't rubberneck around and try to identify him now. If the accident in St. Louis and its aftermath somehow became a matter of public record, this fellow might be moved to report that he had seen Leland spending more than an hour on the flight warming up one of the stewardesses. There was nothing you could do about the way people saw such things. Leland wanted to think that the screwiness had started in the taxi when they turned onto the approach road, but at last he realized that he had been going since early morning after three hard days' work, and he was tense and tired no matter how lucky he had just been with Kathi Logan, and he needed a night's sleep.

Three months after Leland released what he knew of the old botched murder case, Leland's partner Mike went home early one afternoon and found his wife Joan coupled doggy-style with her other high school boyfriend. Leland and Karen had expected something like that of Joan, but not with such exquisite timing. Joan was one of those connivers who worked hardest against those who were wise to her—like the Lelands, for example. Leland and Karen were still formally separated at the time, but that was having less and less effect on their lives with each other.

Leland did not know it at the time, but the agency was

18

ready to break out nationally. For as long as they had been in business together, Leland had been free to develop new business while Mike handled the books and ran the agency day-to-day. Now Mike was an emotional wreck. It took Leland another year to see that his case was hopeless, and by then Mike was beset on the other side, too, being sued by Joan. Leland wanted Mike out, but it cost two years' earnings, with Joan and her lawyer getting nearly all of it. In eighteen months, Leland negotiated seven different loans, wheeling his assets and factoring accounts receivable, to keep all his creditors, including Mike, satisfied. Inevitably, he and Mike had a personal falling out. Leland hadn't heard anything of the guy in ten years.

Leland knew he would have done better with Mike if he had not had problems of his own. All through that period, he was under tremendous pressure, counting on his health and his skills to keep from going under. There had always been a limit to what Karen could take. The week he paid off the last of the notes, Leland's mother went into the hospital. His father assured him that she was going to recover, and Leland wanted to take his father's word for it. He had never felt all that close to his mother, but when she died within the month, Leland felt a shock he could not have been able to imagine. That was the year he cleared seventy-three thousand dollars for himself and started reaching for the bottle. He knew what he was doing to himself, but he didn't give a damn.

The pilot reported cloud cover over the L.A. basin, but no rain, and a five o'clock temperature of sixty-five degrees, which caused a gleeful murmur among the passengers. The San Bernadino mountains were on the right, rising above the dirty yellow soup lying heavily in the valleys. Then came the half-dozen truly tall buildings of downtown, all of them ablaze for the holidays. The big sign on the hill was dimly visible, too, newly repaired: HOLLYWOOD. The last time he had seen it, it had read HULLYWO D. He felt himself sinking into the strangeness of Los Angeles. Stephanie had been here more than ten years, and she loved it. She had a pleasant house on a nice street in Santa Monica, but even there at night he felt something eerie in the way the palm trees were silhouetted against the baleful yellow sky.

19

The streets rolled backward under the wings, the landing gear thumped into place, and the 747 chirped onto the runway of the only airport in the world known by the letters on its baggage tags—LAX. Leland thought it typical of the city's character. His seatmate sighed, and Leland looked over: the man was smiling as if he had survived a trial-by-terror. The last time Leland had taken notice of him had been in the cold and darkness of St. Louis, and now Leland felt chilled, as if someone was pursuing him.

... 6:02 P.M., PST ...

"MR. LELAND?"

It was a black man, elderly, with a graying moustache. He was in livery, including billed cap and black tie. "I was sent to pick you up, sir."

"Today—tonight? It wasn't necessary. You should be home with your family."

"Oh, I'm getting paid, sir," the man said with a smile. "Ms. Gennaro wants me to take you to her office."

That was a change. "I have to pick up my luggage."

"I'll take care of that, sir. Just let me have the tickets."

Leland wondered why Steffie had bothered with this. There was no pleasure in it, especially when it led to a seventy-year-old hefting his suitcases. "Come on," he said. "Maybe you'll be home early enough for Christmas Eve."

"That's all right, sir."

It took another twenty minutes to pick up the two bags, and another ten to get the big black Cadillac out of the parking area and into the flow of traffic eastward. The driver flooded the car with conditioned air and burbling stereophonic sound. Leland asked him to kill both. The motels on Century Boulevard extended season's greetings—or so the marquees announced. Leland closed his eyes and hoped that Steffie hadn't cooked up anything too strenuous tonight. She had told him more than once that he was becoming cranky, but the simple truth was that he was not completely in accord with the way his daughter lived these days.

She was assistant to the vice president for international sales, Klaxon Oil. It was a jawful of title, but the job was just as big, and paid plenty. Leland estimated that his daughter was making well over forty thousand, plus bonuses. The problem was that she lived all the way up to it, with a big BMW, three vacations a year, and more restaurant accounts, club memberships, and credit cards than he thought it possible to keep track of. It was her life, of course, and he kept his mouth shut, but he was sure she was overdoing it. The kids were well cared for, and given what they had been through, they were doing better than Leland might have reasonably expected. He loved them and sent them gifts all around the year, but he understood that he knew them hardly at all, that their everyday lives were completely beyond him.

The distance had a lot to do with it, and the times in which they lived.

Not to mention times past, and what he and Karen had brought on their own family. Steffie was away for her first year of college when he and Karen went into their final torment. He had never really understood the long-term dynamics between them. Early in their lives Karen had let herself get in serious trouble instead of coming to him. He thought she had been afraid. They had been separated for years during the war; they were never able to grow back together again the way they had been when they had been young together. They had changed and had gone on changing, never acknowledging their separate frustrations and resentments. He had consciously kept them to himself, and she had believed that she had to do the same. Of the thousands of mistakes he had made, the worst had been in not paying attention to the person she really was.

"I can't go on like this," she said one night, glass in her hand, for it was a time she was drinking with him. "I'm sorry, Joe, but I've been over and over this in my mind, but there is absolutely no way I can tolerate another minute of it. You're not the person I thought you'd be when I met you. It's not that I don't know who you are anymore. I know who you are, a businessman out of town half the time whose work is so secret or esoteric that he won't or can't discuss it with me, if I cared. But can I care—about whether unauthorized personnel have access to the computer? Or if the police force in Prefrontal, Nebraska, is up on the latest in crowd control? Joe, I know it's not shit, but as far as I'm *concerned* it *is* shit, and I'm sick of it. I'm sick of you unable to function at night because of it, and I'm sick of waiting for the future

22

that never comes. I want you out. The sooner, the better. It's not just that I don't approve of you, it's that I don't even like you anymore. There it is. The sex, when it comes, only makes me want to kill you. Get out, Joe. Get out now."

He was drunk before dawn, and he was never sober more than eight hours at a stretch for the next two years. At times, he was genuinely ugly. He called Karen when he was drunk, believing he wanted to plead, but really waiting for the chance to resume old arguments. He had a lot to account for. A marriage as old and bad as theirs was no better than a haunted house, and the two of them found rooms upstairs that had not been visited in twenty years. They fought about them, about who caused what, and when.

Stephanie heard all of it, from one or the other. She flunked out of school, called them from Puerto Rico. It wound up with Karen putting her in therapy and Leland throwing up blood for two weeks in the effort to convince himself that he was doing something that was killing all of them. The next time Karen saw him, he was sober—but in the knowledge that the marriage was over, and that he had to figure out his life anew. He never touched Karen again.

Who could have known she would be dead in less than another eight years?

He had been to the Klaxon building before, a forty-story vertical column on Wilshire Boulevard, and he was familiar enough with the city to know that the old driver was taking the glamour route, north on the San Diego Freeway to Wilshire, then east through Beverly Hills, past the shops and hotels.

As well as the rest: the motionless palms, the glaring billboards. Ninety percent of the buildings in L.A. were low-lying two-story residences and businesses. There was real civic pride in Los Angeles, resulting in some of the most beautiful residential neighborhoods in the world, but there was also another factor contributing to the look of the city, the gaudy, screaming money madness that had hold of Stephanie, and it led to such gross public insults as pizza shacks with signs that leered: "Had a piece lately?" At its worst, you came away with the conclusion that, if the

23

billboards were removed, the power lines buried, and the business signs restricted to a modest size, the city would look like a shaved cat.

The problem was the newness of the place. As recently as the nineteen fifties, most of Los Angeles and its suburbs lay undeveloped. A dozen years ago, when Leland first started coming here, critical stretches of the Freeway remained to be built, and the city was still in fragments. Now Los Angeles was the first postindustrial megalopolis, the giant city of the future, lying in an infant's sleep under a churning, poisoned sky.

"Do you live in Los Angeles?"

"No, sir, I live in Compton, California."

Californians liked to say the word. If he had been in New York or Chicago, the answer would not have been "Valley Stream, *New York,*" or "Cicero, *Illinois.*" It was as if people here wanted to assure themselves that everything was where it was supposed to be, as if someone could tear it up overnight.

As a police problem, the place was a nightmare. If the size and sprawl of the city were not enough, Los Angeles was the only city Leland knew that was bisected by a mountain chain, the Santa Monicas, running from east to west and encompassing such communities as Bel Air, Sherman Oaks, and Studio City, as well as the separate, surrounded city of Beverly Hills—among others. In many areas, ground patrol had proved ineffective, and so the police had taken to the air, in helicopters. It worked. You could run from someone hammering above you, but you couldn't hide.

The limo was off the Freeway now, heading east on Wilshire through the fashionable neighborhood of Westwood. Bel Air rose to the left, hidden in its money. For the next five miles, million-dollar homes were not unusual. In this town people who had never had money before were suddenly truly rich, and they didn't care what they paid for the things they wanted. Rolls-Royce did better here than in India in the days of the Raj. And money was pouring in from all over the world, as old regimes collapsed. In a few years Los Angeles was going to be the most expensive—and corrupt and dangerous—city on the face of the earth.

"What are you going to do for Christmas?"

"I think I'm going to watch a whole lot of TV. My boy built me one of those big-screen sets—you know, with the projector."

"Is he in electronics?"

"No. This is my youngest boy, he's just twenty-one. He's an actor, but he's real good with his hands. He got an ordinary TV, a lens, and a screen, and there I am. Four feet across, just like a movie. The Rams will look big in defeat this year. I'll tell you, this old world is turning into something else."

Leland said he agreed and let the conversation die. He had had enough glimpses of strangers' lives today. It was a comfort to know that the younger generation was no more in awe of the new technology than his had been of Model A's or biplanes, but Leland thought he saw important differences. The old technology got people out into the world and into contact with others. This stuff was for *consumers* locked in subdivided little warrens, people who lived like cattle being raised for slaughter.

People themselves were different out here, eccentric like the English, exuberant in exploring new permutations of themselves. Hula Hoops came from this part of the world. The skateboard. Drive-ins. There were people here so in love with what they had invented for themselves that they spent Christmas every year sunning themselves on the beach. Never mind that the water was too cold for swimming.

Wilshire was all but deserted. A car crossing here and there. A woman yanking the leash of an ugly, forlorn dog. Christmas decorations. Block after block of lush store displays, through Beverly Hills and back into the darkness of Los Angeles again. He was beginning to feel as if he belonged here. A truck was parked alone at the curb two blocks from the Klaxon building, the only vehicle on the block. The lights changed and the limo came to rest across the street from the front entrance.

"Mr. Leland, you go in the front and I'll take your luggage down to the garage to Ms. Gennaro's car. Tell her the keys will be tucked under the front seat—she knows. And you have yourself a Merry Christmas, all right?"

"Sure. You, too—but don't ruin your eyes."

"Right." He grinned, happy with a loving son. "Right."

Leland noticed something on the far corner, nosed in at the curb. It was a big Jaguar sedan of the kind he had owned, to his regret, in the late sixties. The car had been nothing but trouble for Leland, and as much as he'd wanted to enjoy the car, he'd had to get rid of it. This one was in perfect condition. Someone was sitting inside. CB antenna on the trunk. The limo moved forward, into the light of the entrance of the Klaxon building.

Leland said good-bye to the driver and went up the flight of small steps when he thought of the car again and looked back. The man behind the wheel had the CB microphone up to his face—and as far away as he was, he saw Leland looking back at him and tried to get the microphone down. Leland had seen something he shouldn't have, but the trouble was that the other fellow thought that, too. Leland kept going across the small, raised plaza to the glass doors where an old white guy in a gray uniform sat at a desk reading a paper. Perhaps coincidentally, but certainly interestingly, he was out of the line of sight of the Jaguar. The old man saw Leland coming and got up and unlocked the door.

"My name is Joe Leland. I'm expected. Are you an ex-cop?"

"Yes, sir."

"So am I. I'm going for my wallet."

The old man read Leland's identification carefully. "New one on me, but I've been out of uniform fifteen years. Looks good, though, with a nice, raised seal. I know you're expected. What can I do for you?"

Leland told him about the Jaguar. The old man blinked and looked out toward Wilshire, although there was nothing to see from this position.

"There's a jewelry store across the street, and a kind of mom-and-pop combination liquor store and deli. Everything's closed tonight. I'm going to call it in. You take the elevator at the end, thirty-second floor. I don't know what the hell's the matter with people these days. Remember when Christmas Eve was a night off, and all you got was a stabbing or two?"

"Sure, and when you got there, the murderer was sitting in a chair, still telling the victim how wrong she was."

26

"An old-fashioned Christmas."

"They're running light tonight, aren't they?" Leland asked.

"If people knew how few cops were actually working some nights of the year, there'd be hell to pay. If you were armed, we could roust him ourselves."

"Lay off," Leland said. "How many kids are there working the holidays, all of them needing a good collar? I think I'll watch it from upstairs. I'll be able to see it, won't I?"

"No, the party's around the other side of the building."

"Party?"

"Something special. They put something over on the Arabs or somebody. The place is full of young cunt, kids, everything. I gotta make that call before that turkey out there goes gobble, gobble, gobble."

The old man did the gobbles in falsetto, and Leland was finally figuring out that he had been doing Gary Cooper in *Sergeant York* when the elevator doors closed and Leland snapped his fingers and said, "Damn!" out loud.

Who had been on the other end of that conversation with the son of a bitch in the Jaguar? Where was he? You don't need a radio to knock over a deli—or a jewelry store, either, for that matter. What were they up to?

LELAND REALLY DIDN'T know how Steffie had gotten this job. She had come out here with Gennaro, her husband, after college, at a time when she was not on speaking terms with her mother and her relationship with her father was only beginning to mend. Gennaro had looked like Leland, trim, with close-cropped, dark hair—this shortly before the hair explosion. Leland's own hair had been almost completely gray then, but there was no mistaking what was going through her mind, however unconsciously. Gennaro was a bit too eager to make an impression, one of those kids determined to look you in the eye when he was talking. Cops took that as a sure sign of a liar, but Leland was in a period of compromise with himself, he thought, and what the hell, a marriage was a step up for Steffie, even one that was so obviously a first marriage.

They were going to California, Gennaro told him. He had an M.B.A. and a couple of remote connections made in college, and he was "working with the draft board," as he put it—what the hell, Leland said to himself, figuring his influence with his daughter was nonexistent anyway.

Now Leland didn't even know if Gennaro was making his child support payments. For a while he was living with an actress in Malibu, going to all the right parties, and then a few years ago Steffie told Leland the guy had a place in Encino, wherever that was, south of the boulevard, which was supposed to mean something, too. At the time, according to Steffie, he was trying to be a better father to Judy and Mark—malarkey, because Leland hadn't heard either one of them mention their father in all the time since.

Leland began to hear something faintly as the elevator

approached the thirty-second floor. The doors rumbled open and he was hit by a blast of thumping disco. Strobe lights flashed against the walls. Jesus, Stephanie wanted him to find her in this? Did she have the kids here? A half dozen people had spilled out here into the corridor, holding drinks, passing joints, and writhing to the music. Beyond them, in what looked, in the dark, like the whole southwest quadrant of the building, fifty or sixty adults and teenagers flailed to a sound so loud, so acoustically true, or both, that it made the prestressed concrete floor vibrate like the loft of a barn.

"Hi," a blonde said, "Merry Christmas. You smoke this crap? It's good commercial Colombo."

"The doctors at the sanitorium told me not to. Do you know Ms. Gennaro? She wanted me to meet her here."

"Do you know what she looks like?"

"Always have. I'm her father."

"Jesus. I'm sorry. Excuse me. Wait a minute." She ankled out to the middle of the corridor. "You see that door over there? Mr. Ellis's office. The last time I saw her, she was in there with the other big wheels. Oh, Christ, excuse me. Hey, forget I said that, huh? Please. Tell her Doreen said Merry Christmas—and congratulations."

"What for?"

"This!"

"What's *this?*"

"You don't know, do you? Mr. Ellis and Ms. Gennaro just put over a one hundred and fifty million dollar deal! Hey, go find out! Let her tell you—then come back and join the party! We'll take care of you!"

"I'm too old for your mother!"

"But not for me, you old fox!"

He winked and blew her a kiss.

"That's Gennaro's father," he heard her say, giggling, when he was supposed to be out of earshot. He didn't look back, because he didn't exactly like the way she had said his daughter's name.

The desks in the big room had been pushed back against the walls to create the dance floor, and Leland had to elbow his way through the onlookers who were three-deep most of the way around. Ellis's door led to his secretary's office, but the furnishings here were a big step up from the brightly

29

colored metal and plastic outside. Thick green carpeting, rosewood walls, and an imitation stained glass ceiling fixture, all for a secretary. Like everybody else, the Klaxon executives took advantage of tax-deductible, business expense provisions in the revenue code to fit themselves out with the kind of accoutrements that would make a pharaoh's jaw drop. The door to the inner office was ajar, but the thumping of the music vibrating beneath his feet did not let Leland hear anyone on the other side. He rapped his knuckles on the doorframe.

"Who is it? Come in."

Three men turned in their chairs. Steffie, beyond them on the sofa, leaped to her feet.

"Daddy! Merry Christmas! You're just in time!" She rushed across the room, hugged him, and kissed his cheek. In his arms, she felt too soft and out-of-condition to suit him. With her arm around his waist, she turned to the others, who were standing now, and introduced him. Ellis, behind the desk, was in his forties; the man Leland's age was a Texan named Rivers, executive vice president for sales; and the boy in his twenties, Martin Fisher, was Stephanie's new assistant.

Rivers was the first to shake his hand. "Welcome, Mr. Leland. A pleasure and an honor. We heard about your accident in St. Louis. Well, it doesn't look like much." Stephanie looked at his forehead. Rivers turned to the boy. "Do you know how many German planes this man shot down?"

"Oh, yes." He was looking at Leland, trying to match what he had been told to the man standing in front of him.

"It's ancient history," Leland said to him. "Your parents don't even remember it."

"Not true," Ellis said, stepping in front of the desk, smiling. "Not true at all. Welcome. Perfect timing. This is the biggest day of our lives." He pumped Leland's hand with an unpleasant energy that put Leland off at once.

"I heard something about one hundred and fifty million dollars."

"That's right," Ellis said. "It's the biggest contract Klaxon has ever done outside of petrochemicals."

"We're in the bridge-building business, Daddy. In Chile."

30

"Show him that watch," Ellis said to her.

"He'll see it later," she said.

"I've got a model of the bridge upstairs in my office, Mr. Leland," Rivers said.

"Call me Joe. I feel old enough without a graybeard like you treating me like Santa Claus." Or Lucky Lindy, he thought, as images of the past few hours rose in a flurry, stirred like leaves in a wind.

"I was in the South Pacific, myself," Rivers said.

"The whole thing should be put on bubble gum cards, as far as I'm concerned," Leland said. "Stef, I'd like to clean up a little, if I may. It's already been a fourteen-hour day. I'd also like to use the telephone."

"Something wrong?" Rivers asked.

Leland shook his head. He was thinking of the old cop downstairs, but what he had seen on Ellis's desk, a rolled-up dollar bill, made him want to be cautious. "I want to call San Diego." Leland gave Steffie a smile. "Something nice happened on the plane."

"Old goat," she said. "You took the through flight to San Diego, didn't you? She won't be home by now."

"The lady has an answering service or a machine, one or the other. She didn't say so, but I'll bet on it."

"Being a policeman is like having a sixth sense, isn't it?" Rivers asked.

"More like a way of putting things together," Leland said, not looking at Ellis.

"Who *is* this?" Stephanie asked, pulling at Leland's jacket.

"The stewardess," Leland told her. "Don't worry, she's older than you—though not by much. What's this about a watch?"

"I bought myself a present. Why do you call her a stewardess?"

"I usually call them flight attendants. In this context, I wanted it to be clear that I was talking about a woman."

The male laughter made her blush.

"We all hear this," Ellis said. "We're all getting reprogrammed."

"*De*programmed," she said with a smile. Leland turned to Rivers.

31

"I'd enjoy seeing that model later."

"Sure thing."

Who Stephanie slept with was her business—she was old enough to know that office intrigues usually led to trouble—but Leland didn't like the idea of cocaine. Beneath his salesman's gloss, Ellis was as grisly a specimen as Leland had ever seen. Stephanie still seemed incapable of learning the lesson of her life, and Leland could only accept the burden of his failure with her. He gave her another hug. "I'll use your office. I know where it is."

"I'll come with you," she said. "We weren't doing anything but patting ourselves on the back."

"She's the one," Rivers said to Leland. "She put a lot into this. It wouldn't have gone over without her."

"That's just great," Leland said.

In her office, diagonally across the building from the party, Leland went to the window and looked down into the street. The Jaguar was gone. Leland had scared the fellow off, or made him change his plans.

Judy and Mark were here, lost in the crowd and darkness. The party had been Rivers's idea. The call from Santiago had come in this morning, and the place had gone wild. The deal had been very complicated, negotiations with the ruling junta had been delicate, everything was still secret. Klaxon had had to keep her in the background because of the *macho* factor, which made her angry. Rivers had assured her that her bonus would be "just as good" as the others'. She was waiting to see.

Leland thought she looked tired. For years she had been five pounds too heavy, and now it looked like ten. With cocaine in her life, he had to be glad to see that she was still eating. She looked deeply fatigued. Maybe she would be ready to listen to him in a few days. Not now. The first thing he wanted to tell her was how proud of her he was.

"Dial nine to get an outside line," she said. "You'll find everything you need in the bathroom. I'll see you on the other side of the building." Leland waved. First he found the office directory and dialed the main entrance.

The guard said hello.

"It's Leland, the fellow who just came in. The Jag took off."

"Yeah, well, I put the call in. It can't do any harm. He's probably still right here in the neighborhood, and they'll have an easy one. How's that party up there?"

"Deafening. Have a nice Christmas."

"Hell, I'll be here working."

Leland decided to try Kathi Logan tonight, after all—but not this minute. In the bathroom he saw that Steffie knew how to take her perks, too. The place was what you expected to find in milady's boudoir, including shower and fully equipped medicine cabinet. After he helped himself to two more aspirin, Leland took off his jacket and tie, opened his collar, and rolled up his sleeves. He got out of the harness and put the Browning over his jacket. For years he had been able to get away without having to carry a firearm, but then the word had come down. He was a menace to himself and others without a weapon and the practice that would make him effective with it. He had always been an excellent shot, but now, even at his age, because of the practice, he was better than he had ever been in his life.

Leland didn't want to see too much of the Browning with Ellis so close to his thoughts. The rolled-up dollar bill, evidence of cocaine, made the guy clear. An asshole. The LAPD called them assholes, guys who thought they could keep one step ahead of the system in pursuit of their own desperate satisfactions. Steffie was sleeping with him. Leland knew his daughter. She had something of her own to prove—to her mother, to him, to Gennaro, Ellis, and all the men.

In any event, Leland had to be careful. He had steered the conversation away from police work in Ellis's office because of the dollar bill. Marijuana was seen everywhere, especially in California, but cocaine carried very heavy time, and there was no telling how people reacted if they were faced with years in prison. Better Leland play as dumb as Ellis thought Rivers was. What disappointed Leland was that Steffie underestimated him, too—she had forgotten a lifetime of what Rivers thought was a "sixth sense."

Leland didn't like Rivers any more than Ellis, and not because of the old war buddies crap. Rivers was another hustler, like Ellis, only better. A lot of it was the down-home Texas cornpone. Some easterners never got on to that, and it always worked to the Texans' favor.

Texas was a different attitude, almost a different culture. Cleaning the other guy out wasn't enough: you were supposed to look him in the eye, smile, and squeeze his hand. That was Rivers, a sweet piece of work. One consolation: Ellis thought he was as good as Rivers, and he wasn't.

Leland was a traveler trying to wake up, and he washed accordingly, with cold water, deep into his hairline, careful around the Band-Aid over his brow, around the back of his neck, up to his elbows. Then he dried vigorously, rubbing to draw the blood up to his skin. He felt better, tired inside but not yet ready for sleep, good for hours more.

He took off his shoes and socks. In the sixties, the first time he went to Europe on business, he sat next to a German, an executive in the American branch of an optical firm who had crossed the Atlantic over seventy times, going back to the first quarter of the century. Leland said he was working for Ford, doing a study on the economics of shipping parts by air rather than by sea, to reduce the amount of the float tied up in inventory, and then let the old man talk from Virginia to Hamburg.

The old man had known Hitler, whom he called a peasant incapable of reshaping an opinion. The way to cross an ocean, he said, of all the methods he had been able to try, remained the dirigible. One hundred miles per hour at a height of a thousand feet, almost two days in the company of real ladies and gentlemen. A wonderful man, full of wisdom. Leland would have lied, if he had been asked what he had done in the war.

"Do you want to know a secret, Mr. Businessman? You can be wide awake at the end of the day if you wash your feet. Walk around barefoot for ten minutes. You'll feel terrific."

It was true. Wriggling his toes, his cuffs rolled up to his knees, Leland carried his daughter's telephone over to the windows, braced it on his knee, dialed nine, then one, as you had to do in Los Angeles to call long distance, the San Diego area code next, and finally, Kathi Logan's number, which he had already memorized.

It rang twice, then there was a mechanical pick-up.

"Hi, this is Kathi Logan. I'm not home right now, but if you'll leave your name and number after you hear the beep, I'll send you your dime back. Or maybe I'll call you. Who are you, anyway? Wipe that grin off your face and speak up."

Ah, California. Leland was laughing aloud when the tone sounded. Far below, thirty-two stories down, a truck turned from Wilshire into the side street, then just as quickly into the ramp down to the underground garage under the plaza that surrounded the building. Something turned over in Leland's mind. The truck had been going too fast, but that wasn't it.

"Kathi, this is Joe Leland, your friend from St. Louis today. Thank you. Tomorrow build yourself a perfect day. I'm going to call in the evening and ask to see you. I thought we could meet in San Francisco—"

Disconnect. The tape had run out—no, there was no dial tone. The telephone was dead. He tapped the cradle button. Nothing.

He looked at his watch: eight o'clock. Maybe the switchboard had an automatic cutoff. There was no point in going outside to call again; it would only add to her confusion. For a while he stood at the window, staring at the lights on the Hollywood Hills. Someone had once pointed out Laurel Canyon to him—he couldn't remember who it was, or when that had been.

That old German had left one problem unsolved: putting the socks on again. A change in pitch of the air coming through the ventilator made him look up. No, that wasn't it. The music had stopped. Abruptly. He wondered why he would take notice of it, and then realized what he had wanted to remember about that truck: it was the one he had seen parked on the side street facing Wilshire a half hour ago. No wonder the guy in the Jag had wanted to hide the microphone.

The telephone was dead?

35

Leland was going for the Browning when he heard the woman scream.

He was on his feet at once. His head was clear. He got into the harness, drew the gun, popped the safety, and snapped the first round into the firing chamber.

Leland extinguished the lights and opened the door slowly, as silently as possible. The corridor was empty, but now he could hear a man's voice, sharp, but too far away to be intelligible.

Leland had to decide what to do—*now*. His shoes were in the bathroom. If the voice was barking orders to partygoers, then it was only a matter of moments before his teammates made a search of the rooms on this floor. How many of them were there? The staircase was around on the other side of the elevator bank. For a second Leland would be exposed as he crossed the main corridor, but if people were looking the other way, into the party room, he just might get away with it.

The Browning. If he were caught with it, there would be shooting. If he left it behind and they found it, they would come looking for the owner. No time to hide it, either—no sense in giving them the chance to get closer to him at all, not when he was carrying an NYPD badge, whatever its gag origins. Barefoot, the Browning raised, Leland stepped onto the shaved surface of the industrial carpet in the corridor.

The voice became louder as Leland neared the elevator bank. He had to get a line on this, if he could, but he had to achieve safety—some measure of it, at least. He stopped five feet before he reached the corner.

An accent. Leland still could not make out the words. The accent was faint; the careful, conscious phrasing showed that the speaker had studied the language in school, or later. Now Leland darted across the elevator area to the staircase door.

Four of them, one of whom he recognized, goddamn it— god-*damn* it!—all armed with the world's best one-man weapon, the Kalashnikov AK-47 assault rifle. Leland shook with rage and self-reproach. He should have done better than this!

He waited, catching his breath. If he had been spotted,

someone would have shouted. He had to evaluate what he had seen, which was plenty. He had to think. The first obvious point was that he could not take any kind of effective action with the information he had so far. Now he had to make another decision. He opened the door to the staircase carefully, stepped in, and eased the door closed quietly behind him.

He went up, his bare feet taking the cool, rough concrete steps lightly, two at a time.

HE STEPPED OUT on the thirty-fourth floor. Far enough. The main lights were off, and in all directions, through the full-length windows running completely around the building, he could see the city lights twinkling out to the murky horizon, the freeways streaming red away from the city. This floor was different from the thirty-second, wide open, without protection or hiding place. That was all right, for now.

He realized that he was going to have to learn a lot more about the building. It was the building's core that he wanted to understand first. The core was the same on every floor, eight elevators, four on each side, facing each other like square dancers. Right now he could not tell if the elevators were working, and setting one into motion unnecessarily would probably expose him. The four staircases were around behind the elevator banks, facing the four outside corners of the building. The party two floors down was in the southwest. Okay. Going down that staircase would get him closer to the party, but he wanted to do a little more thinking, first.

He walked around the perimeter of the entire floor, looking down into the street. Garage entrances on both side streets, the ramps cutting down through the steps of the raised plaza. The entry level was two stories high, Leland remembered, sheathed in glass, so that all the elevator banks and the building's supporting pillars were visible. Given the size of the building, the underground garage was at least two levels deep, probably three. At the bottom level, or below it, was the heating plant, the electrical control panel, and the telephone switchboard. You could not defend the building from the ground, but above, far above, with the elevators disabled, it was better than a medieval castle. Not even assault troops could retake the place.

The four men in jeans and Windbreakers, armed with Kalashnikovs, had put on the fluorescent lights and herded the crowd into the center of the big room. Leland had not seen Steffie, or Judy or Mark, but he had seen Rivers and Ellis, their hands on top of their heads.

A half dozen people down there would realize that Leland was not in the crowd, if they were calm enough to think clearly. Of them all, Leland probably had the most confidence in Rivers, in spite of what he thought of Rivers's character. Rivers was a survivor: in that, Leland was more certain of Rivers than he was of his own daughter. A long time ago, she had loved and trusted her father completely. In recent years he had seen her grow annoyed with him, thinking him old-fashioned, out of step, superfluous. But this was not her remodeled kitchen in Santa Monica, and because of her position, she was probably in far more danger than she realized. The man Leland recognized was a killer who liked it—who almost certainly wouldn't be able to resist killing someone tonight, simply to assert his mastery of the situation.

Leland decided to go down the southeast staircase to the thirty-second floor. The door was heavy, fireproof, and almost soundproof. The knob turned smoothly and the bolt slid open in silence. He paused. There was no way of knowing if anyone was looking directly at the other side. He eased the door open.

He had a view of a blank wall. But now he could hear the man who was talking clearly enough to make out some of his words. "You people" something. Then something like "the whole world watching."

Leland stepped into the hall. He wanted to see what they were up to. He wanted to see how many of them there were. The hall narrowed into forty feet of relatively dark corridor, and it would take a good pair of eyes in that brightly lighted room to make him out in the shadows. He kept the Browning in his left hand. Even if he were seen, he would be able to get

39

back to the stairwell, and as long as they didn't think he had a gun, they might believe he was no threat to them.

His view was not what he had been hoping for. He could see only one of the gunmen and a portion of the crowd, their hands still on their heads. The leader, the man Leland had recognized, went on talking, making something else clear: he knew he was secure from below. Leland went back to the stairwell and climbed up one flight.

Suspicion confirmed: the thirty-third floor was different from the other two above and below it that Leland had seen, a series of rabbit warrens leading to fair-sized, plush offices at the windows. Some even had television sets. He had to get organized and keep track of things, make a list of the different floor layouts he was encountering. If he had to run for his life, he might just make it because he had an idea of which direction to take.

The gang. He'd seen four. Even with their radios, they needed two people downstairs, in the lobby and in the control room. The one in the lobby was probably sending the police away at this moment. It would take Leland ten to fifteen minutes to get down on foot to the street level from here. He would have the element of surprise in his favor, and would probably be able to get out to the street. Then what?

Leland knew as well as any man alive. He had participated in the secret seminars and conferences that had developed the contingency plans of many of the nation's municipal police departments. This was the real, only and true reason for the creation of SWAT teams. The Symbionese Liberation Army shootout was a case in point. Ex-LAPD Chief Ed Davis had tipped the strategy completely with his so-called jocular response to the problem of air piracy: "Hang 'em at the airport."

The strategy: kill them all.

The Symbionese hideout had been burned to the ground, and all inside had died.

At Entebbe, a hostage was killed by an Israeli paratrooper when he did not obey orders and looked up to see what was going on.

Hostages were secondary. The nature of this wave of international terrorism was the only primary element in the definition of the problem. The lectures, slide shows, reports,

40

psychological profiles, material made available by a dozen governments and another dozen multinational corporations left no alternatives. There now existed a world-wide network of people in their twenties and thirties, some acting independently but most in combination with other groups, orchestrated from and protected in sanctuaries like Syria, Lebanon, South Yemen, and Libya, who had committed their lives to the destruction of social order in the noncommunist world. After that, they would build a revolutionary society, and naturally enough there was sharp disagreement among them about how they were going to do that.

Think-tanks had developed various scenarios of what would really happen, drawing on the revolutions of 1789 in France, 1917 in Russia, the long Chinese struggle, and now most recently in Cambodia and Vietnam: purges, massacres, genocide, counterrevolution, new schisms. One fat little academic, proud to be among the "tough guys" packing so much heat, dropped this pearl: "We figure a thirty-three to thirty-eight percent chance of world-wide anarchy, instead of the fifteen to twenty percent we're running now."

The psychologists were more help, but the psychiatrist with the profiles of five real human beings was the most useful to Leland. These kids weren't all the middle-class snotnoses the newsmagazines portrayed. An Argentinian who grew up in a seven-foot house made of reworked oil barrels, cardboard, and wine crates; a Palestinian raised in a refugee camp in Beirut, in sight of highrise apartments and first-class hotels, but who had lost all his teeth at twenty-two. People who had no reason to live hoped for redemption in death, or through it. These youngsters knew they were going to die; it made them cling to each other. Before a mission, they partied to the breaking point, passing the girls around. The Japanese kid spraying an air terminal with a Kalashnikov, scared as he was, knew that paradise was at hand. They really were the wretched of the earth.

You had to go to Europe and America for the middle-class snotnoses. Ursula Schmidt, the German poetess who celebrated death, the Italian kids who specialized in killing politicians slowly, or Little Tony the Red, from Germany again, who loved the drama of death, made theater of it, straightening the tie of his victim before shooting him in the

41

lapel of his jacket—"pinning the black boutonniere," he called it.

It was Little Tony—Anton Gruber—whom Leland had recognized downstairs.

The professional advice, and the consensus of Leland's colleagues, was that these people were irredeemably insane on the evidence, that no outrage—using rockets on a commercial airliner, hacking off a penis in Zaire, executing a pilot after making him get down on his knees to beg for his life—was beyond them.

On Thursday, the next-to-last day of the conference, when Leland and most of the others reported to the amphitheater for what they thought was going to be a day of dividing and subdividing into committees and subcommittees, they found the room being searched—one more time—for listening devices. Sitting in his seat, papers spread before him, was the chief of a department in the Midwest, a white-haired, lantern-jawed man of nearly sixty, one of the most respected policemen in America, his lips drawn so tightly across his teeth that the blood was hardly circulating. Because of what people thought of him, the meeting was convened in the normal manner and the chairman remarked that he thought there would be no objection if he deferred the regular agenda. Without another word, the floor was yielded. The chief stayed at his desk, hardly raising his head, and started slowly.

"I'm sorry about all this, but I had a long, difficult night. For one thing, I wanted us to be able to express ourselves freely. I wanted to be able to express myself freely.

"The longer I thought about this last night, the deeper I had to go inside myself to find out where I really stood. It just kept challenging me, all the way down. Then finally I woke up: not only was it the ugliest damned mess I'd ever had to face as a police officer, it was also the worst problem I'd ever had to face as a human being."

He turned in his seat and looked up to the younger men in the last rows. "For those of you who don't know me, I rattled doorknobs for eight years and served thirty-three months with the Marines in the South Pacific. I've seen everything—I know how terrible life can be. I've been married for thirty-seven years to the same woman, and I love her more today than I did when I was a boy. We have four daughters, all college-educated, and nine grandchildren. I'm going to get the hell out of here on Saturday because we're having a barbeque for my eighty-seven-year-old aunt. She's my mother's youngest sister, and I think she's decided she's going to die, because she asked for the party. We've shared a lot of life, she and I, and I know she feels pretty satisfied with how far the family has come."

He stood up. "Well, these kids have got me thinking of my family, and what's important to me, because they've made it perfectly clear how they feel about anything that can be manipulated to bring about their grand design. Now I paid very careful attention when the psychiatrist was here, and I can see how those youngsters came to the conclusions they have about the nature of the world. If they're wrong at all about the way things work, it isn't by much. I want everybody to have a fair chance at life just as much as they do, but I not only draw the line at killing for it, I fail to see the connection between the kind of killing they do and the social justice they say they want to bring about.

"They *say*. I've been around—I've seen things like this before. Once people like these children start killing, they can't stop. When they're in charge—*if*—they'll organize trials and secret police, but the killings will go on to become a bloodbath, then genocide—you don't have to be an historian to see that once the world is run by fanatics, fanaticism is the order of the day. You don't have to look at the modern period. The Inquisition destroyed Spain.

"This is heartbreak for me. I was raised to believe that we here in the United States are everybody's children, and we have the responsibility of leading the way to exactly the kind of world these kids say they want. When I got older and was able to travel abroad, I saw the other side of the coin: if we're part of the world family, then what we are dealing with in other countries are our grandparents' cousins' great-grandchildren—the difference between us goes back, in most instances, to the smallest stroke of fate.

"We happen to be here today because the world is in an upheaval so violent that our country, which used to be safe, isn't anymore. It's been a time, my aunt and I agree, when families have had to hold on for dear life. And many haven't.

43

In the past fifteen or twenty years, we've seen many, many lives wasted or destroyed."

He took a step back and hitched up his belt. "Well, late last night I started asking myself, who the hell did I think I was, bringing my personal life to all this? I'm a professional police officer, in charge of a department responsible for the safety of almost a million and a half human beings. Because I'm determined to be professional, I'm burdened by a great mass of law, regulation, and prior practice. For instance, my department has forty-seven pages of regulations on the proper use of force and restraint. Public information—wonderful, because anyone who wants to go to the trouble, can find out exactly where he stands in any situation beforehand.

"I told you I wanted to speak frankly. A bit later last night when I was trying to understand my options and what they would lead to, I remembered my own regulations governing the use of force. My officers are required to take any and all measures necessary to insure the public safety when firearms are being used in connection with the commission of a felony. In any and all instances.

"What the hell are we talking about here? A lovesick ex-husband holding his ex-wife and kid in their house at gunpoint? Three characters hitting a supermarket? Whether the characters in the supermarket know it or not, the last thing we want in a confrontation like that is loss of life. As for me, I don't even think, over the long haul, that it's good for the morale of the department, if it happens too often."

He arched his back and threw his chest out. "These kids aren't a bunch of losers looking for the exit. They're a tightly organized, self-reinforcing cluster of young psychos for whom nothing is too vile, too low, too uncivilized, if it advances the common madness. I for one am not going to allow my community to become their battleground. One way or another, if need be, I'm going to serve notice that any incursion into my jurisdiction is going to be met with the most extreme countermeasures. These people say they're fighting for the future. Well, they'll find no future at all in my neck of the woods. And the result will be that there will be no further incidents, no media publicity, no showcase trials. These lunatics will not become heroes. And no hostages are going to be taken later to effect their release.

"As I say, I've given this a lot of thought. I don't like it. I'm going to have to answer to my maker for it. But these kids have made it clear that they're not going to negotiate, except to move closer to their own goal, not to accommodate anyone else, and I don't need my old aunt to tell me that that most definitely includes my four daughters, their children, and everything my family has worked to accomplish for four generations.

"And it's clear, too, that we'll get no help from the media, who are not to blame. The news is what we make it. If we started parading prisoners in front of the press, the newspapers will tell us what they had for breakfast when they were seven years old—and if they can't find it out, they'll make it up. As for television, all it does is take pictures of what we put in front of it.

"I want this clearly understood. A prisoner is a snarling, sullen, cocky little prick. A corpse is garbage. A person using a firearm in my jurisdiction is going to suffer the results of the most extreme measures. I mean death. If these people come to my community, they're going out on stretchers with the sheets *off*, so that everyone can see *exactly* what will happen the next time. I mean every word I say—God is my judge: I take personal responsibility for this."

He sat down. One by one, police chiefs and their representatives got to their feet and applauded. Leland and the big guy on his right were among the last to stand.

"A lot of innocent people are going to die," the big guy said.

An older man in the row in front turned around. "Ten years from now, five years, those fuckers are going to get their hands on an atom bomb. Do you think they're going to hesitate to use it?"

None of that mattered now. Little Tony, the man downstairs, was one who had been profiled at that conference: Anton Gruber, a.k.a. Antonino Rojas. Little Tony the Red, who straightened neckties, who liked to "present the gift of death" in the form of the black boutonniere.

There was a hell of a lot more that Leland had to know. It was now 8:52. They had been in the building more than half an hour. No gunfire so far, but that was not necessarily a

45

good sign. What was their plan? There were too many of them for this to be a suicide attack. The language Leland had heard left no doubt that, whatever their objectives, they were going public with it—which meant that they planned to take hostages away with them.

Sure, packing them in, using them like insulation, they could get thirty or forty hostages in the truck with them. If they had Kalashnikovs, they probably had fragmentation grenades.

Now Leland realized that he was listening to an elevator humming in the shaft.

HE WAS RUNNING barefoot on the carpet. It sounded as if the elevator was going up, and at the least, Leland wanted to be sure of that much.

Here on the thirty-third floor the elevator bank was lit as though for business hours. He had no problem hearing the elevator, and he got his ear to the door just in time to hear the door of the car rumble open—high overhead.

Forty stories. Seven flights to the top. Figuring ten feet to each floor, seventy feet. Four hundred feet from the street to the top of the building. He was in good condition, he thought; he did ten minutes of sit-ups every morning, and made sure he walked as much as possible, all the year around. He hadn't smoked since he quit drinking. What he knew for a fact about the fortieth floor was that Rivers's office was up there—and the other top executives' offices, too, presumably.

He was in the northwest stairwell again, figuring he would hear the elevator if it started back down. At every floor, he stopped and made a note of its plan. The more information he could gather, the better. That was the least. What was the most he could do? Free the hostages. He stopped at the thirty-eighth floor, which was another with an open plan, to rest.

He could disrupt them. He could see that they were public before they planned. As the doorman pointed out, there were damned few officers of the LAPD on duty tonight, perhaps as few as two or three hundred over the whole city. SWAT was supposed to be ready on a moment's notice, but the team members had to be called individually. The LAPD would need more than SWAT and a captain for this anyway.

47

Leland knew the procedure: within three hours, a deputy chief would be in charge.

And until that time, assuming that Leland had left the building to notify the police, the hostages would be completely at the mercy of the terrorists. Assuming that his continued presence inside would constitute some kind of pressure.

What *could* he do?

If he waited for the elevator to start downward again, then pressed the call button, the car would stop and the doors would open before the terrorists would know where they were, or that Leland was waiting for them.

Even if there were as few as two of them on board, Leland, with his Browning, would have a less than even chance against their automatic weapons.

Suppose he took them, two of them. And got their weapons. The others would figure out from the wounds that it had been one against two.

They'd know Leland had a pistol, as well.

The less they knew about him, the greater his chances for survival. The longer he'd live.

It occurred to him that his chances were best if he did nothing at all, if he just stepped out of it and let events run their course.

But he *could* disrupt them. He *could* get out a signal from inside the building. He *could* force them to direct their attention to him, or whatever they thought he was.

He had that going for him.

And the Browning, with its baker's dozen rounds. They would assume that he was not armed. In fact, the longer he could conceal the existence of the Browning, the bigger it would grow in his arsenal.

At the thirty-ninth floor he stopped to make note of what he had found on the floors below. He had picked the appropriate floor for the storage (and later retrieval) of information. The thirty-ninth contained the Klaxon computer complex, a whole, surgically clean floor of data banks and terminals.

Leland made a little chart, based on observation and deduction.

48

40	Exec. suite—how lux?
39	Computers
38	open—all desks
37	N: pvt. offices / S: open—word processing
36	cubicles—walls and half walls
35	open
34	open
33	cubicles and offices—TV sets
32	hostages

Valuable information, but none of it was worth a damn if he could not get a message out. Leland could see that he was as good as dead if he thought of this as anything less than war. For instance, these people had had someone working on the inside. They had moved on the signal that the last of the arrivals was safely upstairs. Leland was certain that their overall control of the situation reflected nothing but advance information, even if only from a duped secretary, like the one Leland had overheard in the hall.

And that meant the gang knew who was important, and who wasn't. The question was, how *much* did they know? Leland had to assume the worst.

He went up the rest of the way to the top. The stairwell door opened onto a hall that was narrower than those below, paneled with rosewood, and softly, comfortably carpeted. The lights were on. Leland could hear the hiss of the air conditioning, but nothing more. The floor had to be a maze of outer and inner offices, conference, dining, and board rooms, and probably even a small but fully equipped gymnasium.

Leland did not move. What else?

The model of the bridge.

What else connected with the bridge?

Leland had been assuming that all of them were German, or European. What did a Chilean youngster look like? The military junta ruling Chile was the most repressive in the Americas, as committed to torture and murder as Duvalier of Haiti at his most lunatic.

Now Leland heard an elevator again. He was so close to the roof and the elevator machinery up there that he could tell that it was not the elevator that had stopped on this floor, but another, probably coming up. Another question answered: they had not shut down the elevators—yet.

The elevator came all the way up to the top. Leland pushed the door open a little more.

"Wo sind sie?" It was the voice Leland knew.

"Durch diese Türen, ganz da hinten."

Leland's own German was good enough for that: Little Tony wanted to know where "they" were, and he was told to go "all the way to the back." Leland decided to take a chance. He stepped out into the hall and headed in what he thought was the other direction.

The floor was a huge playground of executive privacy and privilege. Leland could see that it was going to be more difficult to find the stairwells on this floor than on those down below.

Leland was on the south side of the building. The president's office, and the chairman's, would be on the north side, out of the direct sun. Given his importance, Rivers's office would be on that side, too. Leland was learning to get his bearings from the lights outside the windows, swimming out from underneath him toward the horizon.

He may have come up a blind alley, Leland realized. He was in a private office, but narrow, small, and windowless, on the inside of the building. The other door was a massive, solid-looking affair. Leland had the Browning out again.

The door was unlocked, the room on the other side unlit. The crack under the door on the far side was as bright as a strip of neon—bright enough to let him see that he was in some kind of reading room, with a table and chairs. The corporate law library. Given what he knew about major corporations, Leland could almost calculate the distance in inches to the president's office.

He could hear something on the other side, at a distance, he thought. The doorknob on this side was fitted with a twist lock. He opened the door slowly, and sure enough, the first

50

things he saw were the raised letters on the other side of the door identifying this room as the library.

He was looking down a long corridor—it ran the length of the building, almost a block, all the way to Wilshire Boulevard. He had come all the way around the elevator bank. He was almost beginning to feel at home in the building.

He had the door open fully when something made him stop and get back inside. At the end of the corridor, a light came on. Leland's heart was pounding again. He must have seen a shadow, he thought. He was going to have to learn to trust himself. Now two men, one of them Anton Gruber, stepped into view and started talking. They were wearing kit bags slung over their shoulders. Leland held his breath so he could hear them. Still, they were so far away that their voices sounded like they were coming over a telephone on a pillow halfway across a room.

"Besteht eine Möglichkeit, dass er uns helfen wird?"

"Ich glaube nicht. Der weiss doch, dass wir ihn umbringen werden, sobald er uns gibt, was wir wollen."

They were talking about Rivers.

"Ich mag das Töten nicht."

"Je schneller wir ihn umlegen, umso leichter wird uns das Töten in der Zukunft fallen, wenn es notwendig wird. Dieser Mann verdient den Tod. Bring ihn jetzt her und wir erledigen das."

Leland waited a moment, then looked out. The feeling was strange beyond all believing. Through the looking glass. Leland had been thinking it all evening, since—when? Gruber had a Walther. He wanted to kill somebody, like a kid— that much the briefings had right. He had Rivers in front of him, and Rivers was it. Gruber dusted imaginary lint off Rivers's shoulders. Rivers didn't believe it—he didn't exactly know what was going on. Gruber put the muzzle of the Walther on Rivers's lapel and pulled the trigger. Rivers had a split-second of incredulous horror as the shot was fired, and then he was dead, sitting down and sprawling back with a little bounce, like a load of wash.

Now Leland was running for his life.

He stopped when he got to the thirty-fourth floor—he wanted a wide-open floor. Through the looking glass, like it or not. The city floated out below him, serene and twinkling on Christmas Eve, with Rivers dead on the fortieth floor, his heart looking like a piece of stew beef. The shock, they said, stunned you senseless before you hit the floor. Hunters said that. A deer hit the ground as if it had been thrown off a truck.

Through the looking glass: he had thought it first in St. Louis, at Lambert Field succumbing to the snow. Officer Lopez, who should have been in Los Angeles. Leland hadn't found the marshal on the airplane, just Kathi Logan. He'd wanted to get back on the plane. You never listened to yourself.

Leland had seen it on Rivers's face. He'd had a fraction of a second to realize what was going to be done to him. After Rivers was Ellis, then Stephanie. What Ellis was worth depended on how long it took him to realize that Rivers was dead. Ellis couldn't help them upstairs anyway: his office—and presumably his authority—was on the thirty-second floor.

It was 9:11.

Gruber and friends had been in the building over an hour.

Taking stock, making a plan: Leland couldn't send a signal without expecting to be detected, which meant that he would be drawing one or more of them toward him. Could he make them underestimate him? Then what? If they made one mistake, could he draw them into making another? If he could, would he be able to capitalize on that, too?

And he would be proceeding without knowing if his original signal had gotten out in the first place.

He was trying to devise a strategy that would give him not just the advantage, but the momentum. He knew what all the floors looked like, and if he forgot, he had them noted on his piece of paper, like a college crib sheet.

And if he got past the first step, he would have another means of communication at his disposal—not to mention destruction. He wanted to get his hands on one of those Kalashnikovs.

Later for that: now he would settle for a knife.

He wasn't going to find a knife, but, probably in the first desk he opened, a pair of scissors. No flashlight—that would

52

be in the basement, or in a supply closet. Every floor had fireaxes. And hoses. He wondered if he could check the pressure. There were other things as well—he sensed his imagination warming to the problem. Oh, yes, the looking glass. He had not taken the step. It had been taken for him, on the fortieth floor, by a gladhanding asshole named Rivers.

A pair of scissors. He wanted to cut some electrical wire.

HE WAS ON the thirty-fourth floor again. He had been to the thirty-fifth, with its similar layout, and had it ready. Now that he had this ready, too, he suffered a loss of self-belief. One good shot and he was dead. Was he ready for that? More ready than Mr. Rivers, ennobled on the deep-pile broadloom upstairs. Leland had seen many corpses, and he had seen men die, but he had never seen a man shot to death in cold blood. Plugged. In all this, Leland had forgotten pointing the Browning at the man-mountain driver of the station wagon in the snow burying St. Louis. He wondered how the cab driver was doing. He was home with his family, so Leland was going to stop worrying about it.

His plan was not going to work. But he had to try. He couldn't let them know he had a gun. He had discovered he could flash the overhead fluorescent lights in code while watching the elevators. The stairwell doors were rigged with fireaxes to set up a clatter if they were opened. At the first sign of someone approaching, the lights would go out. There was nothing subtle or elegant about it. He was waiting to see how many of them he was going to catch.

He was facing the Hollywood Hills. What did they see from up there? This building stood alone, with nothing around it rising as high as ten stories. The word KLAXON, in heavy, drawn-out capital letters, banded the roof: from a distance, the letters blended into a band of fluorescence. Lights were on all over the building. The lights of the thirty-fourth floor; flashing three long, three short, three long, would look as thin as a matchstick, almost indistinguishable from the background. And it was far from certain that the flashing would not be seen inside the building. You could see a faint flicker on the rooftops far below—but even if you were looking at it, you might not realize what you were seeing.

The lights disturbed his eyes—he had to fight to keep his mind from wandering. If you believed the popular magazines, for instance, the people living on those hillsides were about the last you would turn to for help. Leland imagined some whacked-out young actor in a Jacuzzi thinking he had picked up on the lights of a Christmas disco. *Hey, dig it*. Karen had always thought he sat in judgment on such people. Never.

They reminded him that what he did was not so important after all. There was a certain kind of life that went on in spite of politics and perhaps civilization itself. Karen had never believed that he could see the connections between whacked-out actors and the disconnected people on his own side of the line, like the doorman downstairs who had come alive with the prospect of rousting the guy in the Jag. The people of Los Angeles spent more money on cosmetics and beauty treatments than any other on earth. That was thought especially funny in San Francisco, where they spent more money on clothes. . . .

Elevator: the humming was like an electric shock.

Lights out. Leland was down behind a desk, Browning in hand. He had a perfect view of the elevator bank. With a single, thin chime, the white light over the second set of doors announced the arrival of the ascending car. Leland was gleeful. Whether they liked it or not, they even told you what doors they were coming through.

One. Just one; he had a Thompson, for God's sake. Leland had to draw the guy with the antique. The guy was fully out of the elevator now. He was about twenty-five. The doors closed behind him, but the car didn't move. Something else to remember. The kid stepped forward cautiously, his finger on the trigger. Twenty-shot clip. He was still a long shot for a handgun.

"Say, you! You come out with your hands up! We've been watching you flash the lights! Come out, we're not going to hurt you!"

Another German. Leland had to remember not to silhouette himself against the lights outside. He kept low, scuttling around to the west side, making it a long shot even for a submachine gun. What he needed was a paperweight, something twice the size of an ink bottle. The kid was groping for the light switch, still a good twenty feet from it. Now Leland headed toward the stairs.

"Come out! Don't make this difficult for you! We have guns! We are not afraid to use them!"

A flower pot. A little striated philodendron, with nice, white leaves. Leland kept his arm stiff and hurled the pot like a grenade toward the windows of the north wall. Dirt spewed out of the pot across the desks—it didn't sound anything like someone running, but it was enough: the kid was firing five or six shots even before the pot crashed on the floor.

Then something strange happened, a sputtering, popping noise. The windows were splintering. Tempered glass, they were dissolving in a million tiny opaque fragments. Outside air whooshed into the room. The kid moved toward them, springing from desk to desk.

Leland headed toward the stairs—and the light switch.

It was close enough to the end of the wall for Leland to reach it from cover. When the lights came on, the kid whirled, ducked, and fired all at the same time. The recoil knocked him on his backside, and the burst tore up twenty feet of urethane ceiling panels, which jumped out of position and fell down onto the desks. Leland waited until the kid came up again, blinking. The Browning was out of view. Leland was shaking: he had contracted with himself to kill this kid, but now he did not know if he could go through with it, at least on the terms he had planned.

"Hey, shithead, over here!"

Another burst, thudding into the plaster walls. Surely they were hearing this down below. Stephanie and Ellis knew what it was about. Leland ran up the stairs and out across the thirty-fifth floor. He had cut lengths of electrical cord, tied them together, and hoisted a chair draped with computer print-out paper up against the window. It was a lousy effigy, or scarecrow, or whatever it was, and now Leland thought that the kid already had made so many mistakes that he was going to start getting smart. Leland knew his luck

56

could not hold indefinitely. He set his contraption in motion, then ran back for the stairwell.

The thing rotated slowly, catching the light. Leland heard a scrape on the stairs. He was around the corner, not six feet from the door. The kid appeared. He was not fooled. He stepped toward Leland's contraption, the Thompson up, ready to shoot. Leland ran at him, the Browning raised like a blackjack.

The boy almost got around in time. The Browning struck a glancing blow off the side of the boy's head, knocking him backward. He was still conscious, trying to get the Thompson up between them, when Leland hit him again, throwing his weight on him. The kid's head struck the vinyl floor; the submachine gun went flying. The kid got to his hands and knees. He was stunned, trying to crawl away. Leland locked his forearm around the boy's neck. He caught the windpipe. The kid's hands came up. There was no time to waste. Leland got his shoulder against the base of the skull.

They taught this with drawings and diagrams, not demonstrations. "Believe me, it works," the FBI instructor had said, almost a quarter of a century ago, "I hope to hell you never have to use it."

The human spine was as thick as the handle of a baseball bat. Focusing on what he had been taught made Leland lose sight of what he was doing to a fellow human being. There was no choice—not with Rivers lying upstairs. You had to throw your weight out behind you as you dove forward; your shoulder, with all your weight behind it, separated the skull from the neck.

Leland did it, flinging himself out as if from a diving board, and the boy's neck broke with a sound like a sapling being twisted in a strong man's hands.

His head flopped like a chicken's.

Leland felt his bladder open. He thought he was going to be sick. He had to relieve himself. He breathed deeply and held on. He could hear the kid's bladder spilling. The kid's legs were shaking, his hands clenching, as if they did not know they were dead.

Leland retrieved the Thompson and set it on the desk while he went through the kid's shoulder bag. Two more full clips—forty rounds. A small but promisingly heavy hand-held CB radio, civilian America's version of the walkie-talkie. Candy bars—a Milky Way and two Oh Henry!s. No grenades.

Leland pulled the bag off the body and put it over his own shoulder. He would be crazy if he thought he had gained an advantage. He had passed from having been undetected to someone they had to hunt down. They would not underestimate him again.

He had to figure he had used up all the luck he was going to get. He had to figure he was a dead man; he had done it during the war, as much as he had wanted to live. It had been the thing about him that Karen had understood least. You forgot you had a personal destiny. Yes, when the mind and body were together, functioning as one, you forgot you had a personal identity. That was the trick of it.

He rolled a secretary's chair next to the body and then wrestled the body into it, struggling to get the weight onto the seat. The head hung face-down on the chest, almost face-inward. Leland scavenged the remaining cartridges from the clip on the Thompson, then fitted a fresh clip. He took paper and a marking pen from a desk.

When he was ready, he wheeled the body around to the elevator bank. It was the second car that had come up to the thirty-fourth floor; if it had not been called back down, it would travel up one flight in only a moment. Leland touched the button and ducked around the corner.

The chime sounded almost at once, and when the doors slid open, the car was empty. Leland braced his foot against the door while he rolled the body in and turned the chair around.

Now he looked up. This was the thing he had wanted to see, if he could climb to the roof and replace the panel before the car reached the thirty-second floor.

Using the muzzle of the Thompson, Leland poked the panel aside. The gun would have to go up first. He could gain six to ten seconds by pressing the buttons for the thirty-fourth and thirty-third floors. The question was, did he have enough strength to pull himself through the hatch? If he didn't, the doors would open and close on the thirty-second—he would have thirteen shots to defend himself for three to five seconds.

He reached up, got a handhold and lifted himself up to his toes with one hand. He pushed the Thompson up, touched all the buttons, and allowed the doors to roll shut.

He was on the roof when the car reached the thirty-third floor, but he was still trying to get the panel back in place when it started down again, and he was just getting to his feet, the Thompson slung over his shoulder, when the doors opened on the thirty-second.

They were waiting. A woman gasped—they had women, as he had suspected. The car shook as people stepped aboard and the doors started to close again before they were blocked. Leland could see only a narrow strip of floor no more than a foot out from the elevator entrance. He was aware of the shafts on both sides, but he saw no reason to get curious and look down.

"Was geht hier vor? Lass mich den Zettel sehen!"

Little Tony again, wanting to know what was happening. " 'Now we have a machine gun,' " he read. "His neck is broken?" he asked. "Speak English."

"Maybe a security guard we overlooked?"

"Why would someone do this if he had a gun? The note says, 'we.' That's interesting. What did you find in that office?"

"A jacket, shoes, and socks."

"One man's clothes. We? A man and a woman, if what you said is true. They went off to make love and were able to slip away. Upstairs? Why is the man without shoes or socks and the woman fully clothed? Lovers who break a man's neck like a Green Beret? Oh, no."

"We have to do something."

Little Tony the Red sighed. "We have to tell Karl his brother is dead. I want Karl down here. The body should be upstairs, out of sight. I want these people kept calm for as long as possible." He moved almost out of earshot. "Call Karl on the radio and tell him to come down here. When he is on the way, you and Franco take Hans up to that place where we put the other fellow. This individual—or these people—now have one of our radios. That is not on the note.

59

This was not braggadocio and the man is no fool. You and Franco come down via the stairs with your weapons cocked. We will keep the way clear for you."

"Karl is coming down," a new voice said. "You had better get going."

The doors rumbled shut, and the car started up. Leland thought of killing them right now, shooting down through the roof of the car, but too many factors argued against it. The shots would be heard. The car might be damaged in a way that could trap and kill him. Or he could not be as effective against these two as he had to be. Perhaps they were doing him a favor, taking him all the way to the top.

Now the car coming down rushed past him so quickly that he had to reach for the cable with his other hand. He spent the rest of the trip holding on tightly.

He waited until they were wheeling Hans out of the car before he took the step up to the catwalk inside the elevator shaft above the fortieth floor. He had to climb over a double railing. He was smeared with heavy, black axle grease. Unless he could clean up, he was going to have to be careful reaching for hand or footholds. When the elevator door closed again, he was left in darkness.

A bit of light came through a ventilator. Four elevators on one side, four on the other: what was in the middle? The wall was concrete. He felt his way along until he came to a metal door four feet high. In the center was a sheet-metal sign he couldn't read. Warning enough, he thought. The door swung outward heavily. Leland took one of the .45 cartridges from the canvas bag and held it out through the door opening before dropping it. Thirty-two feet the first second, double that second, double again the third. After almost four seconds, the cartridge landed with a nonexplosive clatter. All the way down. He'd found the air-conditioning system. He smiled. All he needed was a rope, boots, hammer, and pitons—he could run through the building like a rat. He went on.

There was another metal door at the far wall, this one large enough for a man. It was not locked, but something pulled it closed. The wind. It was howling up here—but by the look of things, blowing the smog out to sea. The city was brilliant. He was looking south to highrises on the horizon twenty or thirty miles away, the traffic still flowing toward them. Long Beach and San Pedro, according to Stephanie. He was two or three stories above the lighted edge of the roof. One thing was obvious: you couldn't land a helicopter up here. You could land assault troops, but you couldn't possibly get the hostages to climb flexible ladders into helicopters hovering forty-five or fifty stories above the street.

Leland went down the ladder to the roof itself. All four stairwells wouldn't come up as far as the roof, but certainly one would lead to a door up here. Leland wondered if anyone else was thinking along the same lines, but there was no reason for anyone to have guessed he had climbed onto the roof of the elevator.

But there was no question about it: in Little Tony, he was up against one smart customer, who had been able to cut right through the nonsense Leland had incorporated into the note. If Leland had any more luck, this individual was going to get to know him a whole lot better, possibly well enough to get even one step ahead of him. Leland asked himself: if he were on the other side, what would he be looking for?

Now he thought he probably had made a mistake, not killing the two in the elevator. They expected him to try to use the radio, and if he allowed them to learn that he had made his way to the roof, they would see that much more clearly how cautious they had to be with him.

It would have been better if the elevator car had arrived on the fortieth floor with three corpses in it. In the confusion, he would have had that much more time to get a message out.

Sure, they would have heard the shots, but if he had been thinking, if he had been willing to take the chance, he could have cut deeply into their numbers, drop back into the car, stop it, and get off before it reached the fortieth floor.

He shuddered, and it made him wonder if he was going into shock. He could still feel that boy's neck breaking. He couldn't let himself think about it. If he caved in, it would be only a matter of time before they caught and killed him. He could not be mistaken about that: if they caught him, they would kill him.

61

He found an open door in the southwest corner. Inside was a large room containing fluorescent lamps for the sign around the roof, and a staircase going down to the fortieth floor. The door below probably opened on the corridor he had followed around the building before he had seen them kill Rivers. If Leland understood the way these people worked, sending Karl downstairs left only one man on the fortieth floor. It was 10:25 now—it had taken him almost ten minutes to find his way down from the elevator tower. How many floors had the other two been able to search? Leland wanted to know what they were doing in the executive suite, but getting a message out was more important. He went back out onto the roof.

The radio had five channels, which someone had helpfully numbered. The selector switch was set on channel twenty-six. Leland flipped the radio on.

". . . so you see it is quite pointless to continue. Unless you surrender to us by ten-thirty, we are going to start shooting hostages. Who knows perhaps we will shoot someone you know and love. . . ."

Bullshit. Little Tony Gruber was taking a shot in the dark. He wanted to keep the hostages calm. He wasn't going to do that by shooting them. He didn't even know if Leland was listening. Of course, if Leland acknowledged the transmission, everything would change, and not in Leland's favor. Something bothered him about this. Even given the fact that he was loose with a submachine gun, why would the guy devote so much time and energy to him?

They weren't ready to go public. They needed what Rivers had refused to provide. On the fortieth floor.

At 10:28 P.M., Leland turned the radio on and pressed the "Talk" button.

"You run your mouth so damned much, I can't get a word in. I want to make a deal with you. Are you listening?"

"Yes. Go ahead."

"Let me send the girl down. She's done nothing and she's afraid something's going to happen to her. Let me send her down in the elevator. I want your word on that."

62

"Yes, of course, you have my word. Summon an elevator and put her aboard—"

Leland wasn't listening. He put the radio down on the table in the law library and stepped quickly into the long corridor leading down to the two bodies and the executive suite. Leland figured he had about a minute—long enough for them to realize that he had distracted them for his own purposes. Who among them was alone? Leland wanted them terrified of him, if that was possible. He was beginning to look terrifying anyway, covered head-to-foot with grease from the elevator cable.

As he reached the end of the corridor, the lights in the suite went out.

Leland froze. He heard a clicking sound, far off around the corner—someone trying to turn a doorknob quietly. Leland took two steps back, then turned and ran. Now he heard them coming. He stopped, turned back, got low, and fired a burst. In the dark he could see nothing, and the roar of the Thompson had him deafened, but he had a sense of the tremendous damage the weapon was doing, tearing through the paneled partition on the far side of the room and the heavy glass plates beyond.

They had figured it out—they had gotten wise to where he was. He backed farther up the corridor toward the library door, and fired another, longer burst. He was shaking now, sure he was going to be shot in the back as he tried to get inside. He ran, stumbling as he reached the door itself, and fell inside.

He was scrambling to his feet, his shoulder going numb from hitting a chair, when the corridor filled with a returning burst of fire. Kalashnikovs—you could recognize their sound anywhere. He had to get his hands on one of those guns. The muzzle flash lit the corridor its entire length, and Leland could hear the damage being done in the rooms on the south side of the building. He was not going to fight it out with them. For all he knew, they were coming around the other way, too. He needed the radio. Given the way the partitions were being torn to pieces, he had to keep low. He scuttled through the far door, the radio slung over his shoulder. He felt like Robinson Crusoe escaping the cannibals.

Across the south side of the building, he tried to keep below the level of the desks, across one small room after another. Three single shots rang out—they were at the library. He kept going, even though he was afraid he was heading right into them again. How had they guessed it? He had done something wrong, but he didn't know what it was. The whole floor was indefensible. If he could get around to the northwest staircase, he could disappear into the floors below.

He held back at the corridor on the west side. Its lights, too, were out. They had been lit before. They were driving him like a deer around the building. This was the bottleneck. They were going to catch him halfway to the northwest stairs, and cut him in half. He wondered if they had learned anything about him from anyone downstairs. There was Ellis, Stephanie's boss. Sure, Stephanie had yet to learn the lesson of her life.

Leland was going to die here, if he didn't get moving.

He took another look into the corridor. The door to the roof was twelve feet away, which was too far, with the radio, shoulder bag, and the Thompson weighing him down. He rapped on the partition separating him from the office opposite the door leading upstairs. Wood, probably three-eighth-inch paneling over a hollow core. If he had the time, he could kick his way through it like a rat chewing through a plaster-board wall.

He looked up: by moving the urethane ceiling panels, he could go over the top.

If he moved fast enough.

On the other side, he had to hang from the metal support and drop the last foot and a half to the floor. He had wanted to replace the ceiling panels, but he had been able to see that they would realize quickly enough what he had done. His shoulder was throbbing now. It would be immobile tomorrow. Firing a Thompson wasn't going to help. He had fired one once before, during an FBI course, and it had felt like trying to tackle Larry Csonka.

The door to the corridor was locked from the outside. He stepped back. He had hoped that he would be able to step from one doorway to the other, but now he couldn't even see the other. When they reached the adjoining room, they would see the hole in the ceiling and understand what he had done to himself.

He had put himself in a box. It was like one of those garden mazes the English loved so much. He was in it and they could blast away until they were sure they'd killed him. Dick Tracy did it all the time.

Unlike the great Chicago detective, Joe Leland had gotten it backwards—and the bad guys had his kid, too, like old Lucky Lindy himself. He wanted to kill them, he thought for the first time. Oh, yes, now he wanted to.

The locking mechanism was covered with that hefty-looking brushed aluminum plate. He had to hope that the ammunition wasn't short-loaded. All he needed was bullets ricocheting around the room, and then the job he would have done on himself would be complete. He moved to the side and squeezed off a long burst. The door swung inward like something out of a ghost story.

Leland decided he wasn't being morbid. Now that he had revealed his position, he had to guess if they were waiting for him at the end of the corridor, or if they had arrived at the next room—or even if they were waiting for him on the staircase to the roof.

Even if he got to the roof, he did not know if he would be able to keep them from coming up after him. In any case, he had no time to think about it. He took a running dive across the corridor, and what sounded like a Browning automatic rifle went off five times, about a foot over Leland's head.

He got up running for the stairs. More shooting. They had enough ordnance to hold off a company of marines, considering the position they held. At the top of the stairs, Leland got low and fired the last of the clip through the open doorway below, trying to buy the time to get out onto the roof. He couldn't hear anything but the roar of the gunfire now. His ears felt like they were crammed with cotton. It would take too long to get another clip on the Thompson. The man with the B.A.R. reached the lower door before Leland got out onto the roof, and for a moment Leland was silhouetted against the pallid sky. Leland dived again, but the man tried to anticipate him, and Leland felt two of the shots pass within inches of his eyes.

HOW MANY? THERE could have been as few as two on the fortieth floor. In his panic, Leland had been thinking at least three. Now it didn't matter. They had him treed like a cat.

He was back on the cool, metal catwalk inside the elevator tower. He'd hoped that he would be all right once he'd gotten to the roof, but it had been nothing for them to ascend the enclosed stairs and cover their own passage onto the roof. By then he had made it around to the iron ladder outside the elevator tower, and when they finally saw him, he was halfway through the door above. Now they could not climb the ladder without exposing themselves, and he had nowhere to go. The elevator that had been on the fortieth floor was headed down. When Leland had peered into the shaft, he had been able to see that they had opened the roof hatch of the car. They had figured out everything, were so close behind him that he had not escaped, he had been delivered.

Leland turned the radio selector switch past channel nineteen to channel nine. He was drawn up in the corner next to the door to the roof, where he would be able to hear them outside as well as watch what was going on in the elevator shaft, for the little it was worth. All they had to do was move their activities to the other bank of elevators, and they had him neutralized. He pressed the "Talk" button.

"Mayday," he whispered. "Mayday. Tell police foreign terrorists have siezed the Klaxon Oil building on Wilshire Boulevard. Many hostages. Repeating. Mayday—" And he went through it again. When he released the "Talk" button, the radio began receiving.

"I doubt that that will be effective. Can you hear me? We know where you are. Will you acknowledge this transmission, please?"

Leland pressed the button. "What do you want?"

"I want to strike a bargain with you, a *real* bargain. These little radios are not very powerful, by the way, so broadcasting alarms from inside an iron cage is probably futile. Are you listening?"

"Yes."

"Stay where you are. We want no more bloodshed. Stay where you are and keep out of our business. We can come after you if we have to. Ah, and you know it won't be possible for us to deal with you lightly."

Leland thought he heard something. "How did you get on to me?"

"You did it to yourself," Gruber said cockily, "when you said you wanted to send the girl down. You heard me say that at the elevator, and you thought I would be quick to believe there was a girl.

"The conversation I referred to in English about the clothing we found—your clothing, I presume—never took place. Possibly it makes no sense to you, but I have found it useful to act on such obscure little impulses. However, now that I consider it, I judge that you do understand. After all, it was you who thought to climb to the roof of the elevator car. Who are you? You are a bold man—"

Why the stalling? Leland had taken the hesitation before the remark about not dealing with him lightly as an indication that the brother of the dead man was asserting himself in unpleasant ways—not exactly a break in discipline, but perhaps a sign. They seemed to have time to burn. 10:50. In an hour and ten minutes it would be Christmas. 3 A.M. in New York. 10 A.M. in Europe. The Pope always had a Christmas message—did he appear in public? The biggest nightmare of the Italian police was an assassination attempt against the Pope. But what did the Pope have to do with an oil company building a bridge in Chile?

Leland rubbed his eyes. He had been awake for the start of "Good Morning, America" in St. Louis, 7:A.M. central standard time. In that time zone it was ten minutes to one, Christmas morning. Eighteen hours. If he'd slept on the plane, he would have missed Kathi Logan, who might be home by now, wondering if her telephone recorder had failed. He couldn't waste time hoping she would make something out of a broken connection. They'd kissed like kids. He wanted to get out of here and kiss her again.

Maybe they were only trying to make him think he was safe. In anticipating him, they'd drawn their perimeter at the fortieth floor. They had been ready for the man who had revealed his presence to them.

Q.: What had he told them about himself?

A.: That he thought he was capable of dealing with them.

Proceeding from that assumption, and the possibility that he was not overestimating himself, they would have to defend what was most important to them. It had taken the leader just seconds to tell the others on the fortieth floor that he was headed toward them. This while he'd been talking to Leland on channel twenty-six. So they had other working channels. Leland was going to have to keep his head up. So far, they didn't know he understood German, however poorly. The radio might become as important as the Thompson.

If he got a chance to use either again.

Another fantasy. Dick Tracy always stitched perfect X's with his tommy gun. It was obvious that Chester Gould had never tried to ride one of these broncos.

Leland did not know if he should try to send another message, or even if it would be worth it.

And he was afraid to open the door and look outside.

Karen would have loved it, he knew. Everything from arriving at the airport in St. Louis to this moment. Pulling a gun in a traffic accident. Kissing Kathi Logan. Letting this happen. And then making one bad decision after another, until he could not make a move, or say a word. Hubris. The All-American Hero. The sin of pride. He'd seen an example of it in an interview with a pretty-boy ballplayer: "My wife was just another co-ed, but then more and more she became a complement to me."

Leland shuddered. He had hurt many people in his life, but he had hurt Karen more than anyone.

Except, of course, for the people he'd killed. He pressed the "Talk" button.

68

"Listen, Fritz, I'm getting fed up with this penny sere-
nade. Suppose you tell me what you bums are up to?"

Gruber laughed. "That's very entertaining. Perhaps you
would be interested in coming down from there and surren-
dering yourself."

"You just told me I couldn't be dealt with lightly. Is Karl
there? Can he hear me? I want to tell him what it was like to
break his brother's neck."

There was a sound, and then the radio went dead. Leland
checked his watch: almost eleven o'clock. He looked at the
door and asked himself if he could really be sure that he
would hear them coming up the iron ladder. He shivered
again. The temperature was dropping—L.A. was a desert
city. He shook.

For a while he dialed around the radio, trying to find their
transmissions to each other, and then he cranked up the
volume and listened to the faint transmissions from outside.
Citizens band. Kids talking about their midwinter skiing
vacations. Utah. One was going back to Arizona. He liked
the slower pace of life.

Leland had to fight the cold. His father, who had been a
cop, too, had taught him to take ten deep breaths; it got
oxygen in the blood, which speeded the generation of heat.
His father had outlived his mother, as he had outlived
Karen. No, not exactly. His mother had had two strokes, a
year apart, and in that year his father had taken care of her.
Karen had been married to somebody else at the time of her
death, which was not the same thing at all.

She died in her sleep, her heart stopping. Her husband
called Leland early that morning, and Leland returned the
favor by forgetting his name. Her husband for two years—
Leland couldn't remember his name if his own life depended
on it. He knew it was a way of not facing what had happened
to their marriage. For all their work, they had let it get away
from them at the end. Failed. Dick Tracy was entitled to
shoot perfect X's: after all, he managed to get the bad guys
in the cubicles, and keep himself outside.

Like a kid counting his Christmas money, Leland checked
his ordnance again. Two full clips, plus extras—more than

69

forty rounds. If he was able to go one-on-one the next time out, he would have a chance of picking up another weapon.

Getting ahead of himself, he thought.

I'm not going anywhere.

After the divorce and before her remarriage, after Leland had quit drinking, and when he had himself in good shape again, Leland wrote to Norma MacIver in San Francisco. They had been drawn to each other years before, but nothing had come of it for many reasons. In the letter he told her what had happened to him. He had been in and out of the San Francisco area on business several times since the divorce, but he had not tried to contact her because he hadn't thought she would like the man he would have had to present to her. Now, he said, he felt better about himself, and wanted to see her.

She called him. They talked for three hours.

Six weeks later, as fast as he could arrange it, he was headed north from San Francisco International Airport in a rented convertible. The weather was brilliant. Norma had an apartment on Nob Hill two blocks from the Cathedral. The key was in an envelope under the mat at the door. The note told him not to worry about the scruffy toy poodle, and that Joanna, her daughter, was due home from school at twenty-to-four. He was walking into another life.

Norma was an assistant to a San Francisco Supervisor, the dog was a jet-propelled little freak, and Joanna was tall and slim, like her father, but dark, like her mother.

"You shot down all those planes, didn't you? My Dad is at the very end of the book."

"He got into the war late. Now that I'm older, I know how brave all of us were, including your father. Especially."

Fisherman's Wharf. Three days later it would be Jack London Square, in Oakland. Norma looked beautiful. Motherhood and ten years had softened and slimmed her; having created so much for herself made her look wise. Joanna was perfect: intelligent, inquisitive, and brimming with self-belief. She knew her mother and Leland would be sleeping together, Norma told him.

No matter. The first time Leland made love to Norma MacIver was in her kitchen, that first night, with the coffee cups moved quickly from the table. He undressed her, more

70

excited than he had ever been in his life, and they made love with their eyes open, under the fluorescent light, looking at what they were doing to each other. He believed he was with the most honest woman he had ever known. He carried her into the bedroom, and in the morning, when they awakened, they were still in each other's arms.

For the next five days they made love constantly, and for more than a year they were lovers, faithful to each other. But she did not want to return to the East, and his business made it impossible for him to relocate in the West. He was wildly in love with her, hoping they could solve the problem somehow, when she suddenly broke it off. She would have been willing to move at once, she told him, if she could have brought herself to believe that she could ever be more than second in his life not just to his work, but what his work represented.

"Joe, if you had once entertained the idea of chucking everything and starting over with Joanna and me, we wouldn't be at this point. But you never said it, never thought it long enough to discuss it with me. I don't want to be in love with a man who would have to fit us in around his career. I won't settle for it. Not even MacIver did that to me—and I don't think you even know what I'm talking about."

He did know. He loved her, but not enough to fully surrender his imagination. A year later she married a Berkeley radical five years her junior and moved with Joanna and him to St. Thomas, in the Caribbean, where they still lived, for all he knew. She had been right. If he had been willing to give himself a chance, he would have been happy. It took him a long time before he could let himself think of her. He still figured that he had missed the chance to salvage something of his life.

"Merry Christmas," he said aloud.

He stood up and stretched, raising the submachine gun over his head. *What'd you get for Christmas, Joe?*

During the Depression, even the cops had been on short hours; you stood on the corner with your buddies a day or two after the holiday, not comparing notes, trying to make your parents look good. "Oh, I did okay. I got what I

71

wanted." He'd been an only child. And he'd had only one, Stephanie. And now Judy and Mark and—for the time being, they were in no danger, he thought.

Hoped.

You didn't tell us, Joe. What did you get for Christmas?

Just what I needed, he thought, in the way he'd talked as a child, *I got this really swell gun.*

Not even his father could understand the things that had happened to him. "Never had to use my gun," he'd said in his old age, as if to atone for the blood on his son's hands. "You don't know how sorry I am that it happened to you."

Hey, Ace, how many kills now?

Leland didn't have any idea. He didn't know how to count the mistakes, like the old cop before the war whose bad idea Leland the rookie had followed in spite of himself, or Tesla, who had gone to the electric chair instead of the real killer.

Karen had helped him with Tesla. "You must not blame yourself. He confessed. The confession was wrung out of him, but not by you. There was a district attorney, a judge, and jury. A defense attorney. You are not responsible."

Perhaps. But because he had survived them both, they danced in Leland's dreams. Tesla especially, living the life that had been taken from him.

Leland put his ear against the door to the roof. Nothing. He peered down into the shaft. All of the elevators were far below, motionless.

The cables were out of reach—and covered with grease anyway. The walls of the shaft were smooth cinder block all the way around, all the way down.

He thought about the door again. If one of them was outside and saw the knob turning, he would have Leland cold. Just touching the knob on this side involved an unacceptable risk.

Whether he liked it or not, he had to take another look at the air-conditioning and ventilating system.

A fellow in San Francisco had fallen down one of these vertical shafts twenty-nine or thirty stories; he'd lived, according to the news story, because the air under him had cushioned his fall. Leland didn't think he wanted to try it.

He figured, too, that he would be wise to make as little noise as possible. If someone heard the little iron door clanging, Leland would have the whole bunch after him again.

He could see about three feet down. The idea of going in the shaft made him so sick, he was not sure he could continue to stand where he was, much less try to sustain himself inside. There was no point in dropping another cartridge. Four hundred feet. This was not the same as flying. It was not even the same as crawling into a cave. The large vertical shaft had to branch off into smaller, but still large-enough, horizontal, rectangular tubes. Once in—if he got that far—he would not be able to turn around. He might not be able to get the leverage to break through the register covering the duct opening. He might find himself head down, unable to move.

Did he have to turn himself into a bug in a drainpipe?

He put down the radio and the Thompson, got on his belly on the iron platform, then projected his head and shoulders through the doorway and down into the shaft.

Wider than he had thought. Almost too wide. He could get down about three and a half feet, no more than that. If he couldn't see the first of the horizontal branches, he hoped he would be able to feel it. No dice. He would have to go in without knowing where the first toehold would be. If it was beyond him, and his strength failed, he would fall to his death. Put another way, he would have almost four seconds more of life, enough to make death far from quick. His stomach churned and he had to back out of the shaft.

He looked again at what he had. How was he going to carry all this stuff? He was going to need both hands, and the Thompson had no sling.

The kit bag had a canvas strap. Unhooked, it extended about five feet. Could one of the hooks hold him? If it could, and if he used the Thompson as a T-bar across the small iron door, he could lower himself into the shaft. Figuring on not being able to extend his arms fully because they'd be bearing almost all of his weight, he could get down perhaps as much as ten feet. If one hook could hold him, so could two—if the first hook failed, that would be the end of it, anyway.

The shoulder harness was thick, top-grain cowhide, and presumably stronger than the canvas of the kit bag sling.

73

Another two feet, with the Browning stuffed in his belt. Another two feet. He might lose the Thompson. As well as the kit bag. No. He could leave the kit bag on one end of the sling, drop it into the shaft, and climb his way down around it, then down the shoulder harness. After he found a foot-hold, if he couldn't shake the Thompson loose, he could still reach up and unhook the shoulder bag. And if he had to give up all that firepower, they would think he was unarmed again—if, of course, he called it to their attention. First, there had to be a toehold.

Don't get ahead of yourself, boy.

He thought. He had been able to step from the roof on the elevator to the catwalk here—step up: he had reached above his head for the railing. It took a little figuring. He could be as little as four or five feet above the conduits in the ceiling of the fortieth floor. Then what? Suppose they heard him scratching around overhead, like a rat inside the plaster?

He had to face the fact that he would go no farther down if he found a passageway at a safe level. If he could not have the relative security of the sling and harness, he would not be able to think about getting in there.

The clips were the weakest links. They could be nothing more than some kind of flattened wire. In the light, they'd looked like brass. He was going to see if he could rig a test, wrapping the Thompson around the railing. No noise. If they heard him crapping around, they would be on their way.

It was a good idea to think of other things when he could. It rested the mind. He wondered about the benefit in talking to himself. He'd thought for years that he'd never done it, but his mother had told Karen that he'd done it as a child. Karen had been an orphan, a foster child. She'd talked to herself. She'd remembered more of her childhood than he ever could remember of his. Since he'd never wanted to be anything but a cop, he'd spent his childhood in a dream world, playing, listening to the radio, passing the time, coming awake to make note of something only when some-one spoke one of dozens of buzz words, like *collar,* the verb, or *suspect,* the noun.

His mother had given him so much support, he'd taken so much for granted, that he'd gotten past the middle of his life,

74

and at the end of hers, before he'd realized how little he understood her. His relationship with Karen had a lot to do with that realization and his father's advancing senility. A lovely woman, his mother, a twentieth-century classic. She'd met her husband right after high school and her only child had been born before her twentieth birthday. She spent the rest of her life creating a home, which an unmarried man knew was making something out of nothing but love, will, effort, and sacrifice.

He stopped to get his bearings again. Even the cartoon Napoleon going out the window of the nut house paused for a check of the knotted bedsheets. Leland was going to know this building—perhaps for only four seconds, but he was going to know it. He made sure the safety was on the Thompson, and then he looped the sling over the railing, which had already taken his weight. The clips still worried him. He was going to be able to put pressure on only the first, there was so little room in here to manéuver. He had to clear his head. He had to think that this was the same as changing a tire.

What would his mother think of him now? The real question was, what had she thought of him before she'd died? She'd always said she was proud of him, but later, when he was being honest with himself, he thought he could recall something else, too. He'd frightened her. Well, hell, he had frightened everybody. All his life, people had kept their distance, only rarely reaching for him.

A parent was entitled to reservations about his or her child, and he doubted that his mother's generation was the first to realize it. He had his reservations about Steffie downstairs. He used to play Monopoly with her, hoping she'd win. There was a lot of real life on Park Place and the Boardwalk.

Now it was cocaine with Ellis. What Leland really knew about drugs had come from Norma, who had started smoking marijuana while he was seeing her. It was the time when drugs first started flooding into the country. He passed; with his track record on intoxicants, he thought he was doing himself a favor. What you made of drugs, like alcohol, was entirely a matter of your personality—and that was what disturbed him about this situation. He knew enough about

75

Steffie and cocaine to see that the stuff could only reenforce everything ugly in her. Cocaine was for powertrippers, people looking for an advantage, an edge—like Ellis.

Like Stephanie. He took a breath.

In. He could not think about his fear. Four hundred feet. The cartridge had taken so long to fall that he had wondered what happened to it. The submachine gun was braced against the bottom of the opening. The door itself was swung wide against the wall, and it was too heavy to swing back to trap the Thompson. Leland thought he was going to lose the gun anyway. The shaft was too wide for him to brace himself across it with his back and feet. He did not begin to put weight on the harness until he was hanging from the opening with his hands. Nothing shifted. Now he was fully inside.

As he hung from the harness, he worked his feet around the walls, probing for an opening. The walls seemed to be covered with some kind of fine dust. He was still within reach of the opening. He had to go farther down, but he didn't believe in it anymore. He didn't believe it would work.

He had to stop thinking: he had no choice.

He lowered himself, one hand under the other, until he passed over the kit bag and down to the middle of the sling. It was too dark to see his hands. He swung his feet around, touching all four sides again. No opening. He had to go lower.

Oh, God, please don't let me fall.

He had about three feet of canvas strap left. Once more, he swung his feet around. On the right, the wall fell away. He had to go lower still, maybe as much as two feet.

No. His foot touched the floor of the horizontal shaft almost immediately. The shaft was no more than twelve inches high.

At least he had something to put his weight on. It was pitch-black in here. What he had to decide was whether he should take a chance on the horizontal shaft. Once he dislodged the Thompson, there would be no way back up.

If the little shaft branched again, he could be stuck in it for days, maybe for good.

He worked his right leg, then his left, into the shaft until he was on his knees, hanging onto the last fifteen inches of the canvas strap. He had to take the pressure off it for the Thompson to fall away from the bottom of the opening. But he was still using the strap for balance.

Take your time, boy.

He dried his left hand on his pants and braced it against the opposite wall. Slowly he released his pull on the strap. From above came a clunk that he felt more than heard. Now the strap would no longer take his weight.

He lowered himself down the main shaft, pushing his legs into the horizontal shaft as far as he could, getting the backs of his thighs against the upper wall. It was as far as he could go without letting go of the strap.

He paused again.

The harness was around the butt of the Thompson, which was supposed to have fallen with the barrel away from the shaft. Now he tugged on the strap. When it gave, he lowered himself more and pushed himself deeper into the little opening. It was twelve by fifteen inches, he guessed: wide enough. He was able to get his hips in so that he was almost horizontal across the large shaft. Even if he could turn his head far enough, there wasn't enough light up above to let him see the position of the Thompson. The safety was on. The whole mess was going to come down on him; he had to get as far into the horizontal shaft as possible when he pulled the strap the last time.

One last pause. He counted backward from five.

He pushed hard with his left hand and wriggled backward furiously; he pulled the strap, something caught and then gave, there was a clang, and as Leland lost his purchase with his left hand and started to pitch headfirst into the shaft, the kit bag hit him on the back of the neck, and the butt of the Thompson bounced off the bag and hit him heavily on the back of the head. He blacked out momentarily; he seemed to know it while it was happening to him. He fell far enough out of the shaft to be able to reach the far wall again. The submachine gun started down, pulling the bag and the strap with it. Leland lunged for the strap as he pushed back into the shaft. His scalp felt like it was bleeding. He had the strap, but he was not safe, and he was still fuzzy from the blow of the gun butt. Using his free hand, he worked his way back until he was flat inside the shaft, his arms out in front of him, his equipment in front of them, the submachine gun still out in the shaft, too long to get into the opening sideways. The top of his head was smearing blood on the metal above, he realized. And he was squeezed in here on all sides. He could feel the rage building inside him as he scrambled forward for the Thompson. He wasn't thinking; he felt his hand on the safety, but he was too angry with himself and his situation to allow the position it was in to register in his mind. His hand went to the trigger, pulled it, and the gun discharged.

THREE SHOTS, SOUNDING like atom bombs in this enclosure, stuffed up his ears tight. He got the gun inside, the barrel pointing away, and reset the safety. He couldn't get the Browning out of his belt. He could turn the radio on, but he couldn't bend his arms enough to get it near his head. He had to leave it between his arms and inch forward to it.

Then work the volume control with his lips.

"Are you all right?" the voice asked. "What was that shooting?"

If he kept quiet, they might believe he was dead, a suicide or the victim of a gun accident. All they had to do was find the nerve to climb the metal ladder outside the elevator tower. Faced with that prospect, they might conclude that it was another trick to get them to expose themselves.

On the other hand, he couldn't be sure of how those on the fortieth floor had heard the shots. For all he knew, they had his position and were on their way. He had to get moving.

He was facing the wrong way. Even if he could see anything at all, he wouldn't be able to see where he was going. He wouldn't be able to see past his own body. He could be backing right into them.

He started pushing his way into the shaft, hauling the equipment after him, moving six inches, nine, sometimes twelve. He had to go fast. He was making noise, but not much; he had to take the chance that there was enough insulation between him and them to mask what they could hear.

There was no way to measure the distance he was traveling. His claustrophobia was almost as bad as his fear of falling, he was beginning to see. Again, he had to keep his head clear. He wondered if there was some way at all to get an accurate count of the members of the gang. He had to forget his fear and concentrate on what was going on here. If they still thought he was up in the elevator tower, it was as good as a new lease on life. He would be able to roam the building at will. He could change his tactics, stop killing, and start counting. As long as they thought that he was out of action, he could send a signal—as many as he pleased.

He came to the end. He couldn't have traveled twenty feet. Something was wrong.

He tried to look around over his shoulder, but it was impossible. No sign of light. The metal grating was cold against his bare feet, and thicker than he would have thought—thicker than such things looked from the other side. He pushed. The thing was really screwed on tightly. The room on the other side would be very close to the north end of the building, which the gang found so important. He pushed again, hard enough for the grating to cut into his skin. He braced himself and pushed harder still, and now he felt one corner part from the wall. He got the soles of his feet in the corner above, and pushed as hard as he could. It was open.

He knew what was wrong as soon as he had his feet down. Tar paper. He had made a mistake. He had figured the distance down the shaft wrong. He was still on the roof.

He drew the equipment out the the shaft quietly. Staying low, he reassembled the kit bag and strap, put on the harness, and put the Browning in the holster. The bleeding from the top of his head had stopped, or slowed, and he was covered with black dust from the inside of the shaft. A few hours ago, he'd been a gentleman in a limousine; now he looked like a circus geek, the guy who bit the heads off live chickens in the sideshow.

He smiled.

He left the submachine gun at the ventilator opening. The roof was covered with pipes and ducts, and he needed his balance getting around to the south side. This time he was going to get a message out, but he couldn't risk it until the roof was cleared. He wanted another one of them, anyway.

Going down the shaft had done it, or running for his life earlier, or maybe it was having to control his claustrophobia in that little duct. It had left him feeling humiliated. Degraded.

But he was glad to be alive. And he wanted to do something to make sure he stayed that way.

The weather had changed. The sky was breaking over the hills, a warm breeze was picking up. He could see snow-capped mountains rising above the downtown highrises. The mountains were forty miles away, he knew Stephanie said that the geography of Los Angeles was the most beautiful in the world, and she was probably right.

Admire the scenery later, kiddo.

He kept low, moving around the elevator tower to the position he thought someone would take to watch the door above. Up here, in the darkness, dirty as he was, he was hard to see. Wonderful. Terrific.

Now his eyes picked up the guy. He was sitting on some kind of aluminum box. Leland took out the Browning, released the safety, stood up, and started walking toward him. It was a moment before the guy looked up, a skinny little guy with wild, wiry sideburns, and for a split second he had that look on his face that said he didn't know what he was seeing, but by then Leland had the Browning pressed into the lapel of his fatigues, the way Little Tony had done with Rivers. The guy's eyes were wide open. Blue eyes.

"You speak English?"

"Yes."

"What the hell are you sons of bitches up to?"

He hesitated, his eyes brightening. He wanted to be smart. He was going to start arguing, or give a speech.

"No time for that bullshit," Leland said, and pulled the trigger. The little man crashed back on the aluminum box. He let out some air and lay still, staring up. "That's two," Leland said. He got out the radio and sent the message on channel nine, the so-called emergency channel, keeping his eye on the door to the stairs into the building. He put the radio back in the kit bag and picked up the weapon in the kid's lap. He was a kid, too, even younger than the first. The gun was a Czech assault rifle, fully automatic. Leland decided to stay with what he had. Maybe the guy had candy bars, too. He didn't have a bag, and Leland was not going to go through his pockets.

The hell he wasn't.

A Mars bar. Leland had always liked them.

He put the gun out of sight behind the box and grabbed the guy's wrist and pulled him up to a sitting position. He had to grab his collar to keep him from falling over.

"When you see what's coming, Skeezix, you're going to be glad you're dead."

Leland slung him over his shoulder and lugged him around to Wilshire Boulevard. The frame for the lighted Klaxon sign extended outward almost a yard, but it also provided Leland with a place to park the body while he caught his breath. He was not going to do any more lifting. After this, though, he wasn't going to have to do anything to get attention, either. He pushed the body over the side.

"Geronimo, motherfucker."

He had to know where it landed. Jouncing him across the roof had pumped the guy's blood all over Leland's chest and back. He had to be sure people could see the body. Leland got his head beyond the sign just as the body struck the steps and rolled toward the street, distorted and twisted as if all the bones were broken. Leland had thought he was too high to hear anything, but the sound came up, loud, an awful, wet, crackling sound. Leland knew at once he was going to be sick. He was back on the roof when he thought of MacIver and all the others who had done that to themselves. They had heard that sound. Leland was able to bend over before the airline dinner Kathi Logan had served him came flying up again.

He spat and wiped his chin on his sleeve. Now to retrieve the Thompson.

He was going to try it one more time. It was the last thing they were expecting. He was careful working his way down from the roof, then around on the fortieth floor to the corridor beyond the library—but he was not slow, either, going purposefully down the thickly carpeted corridor, stepping over Rivers and Number One. He could hear someone working in the board room. He stopped at the left side of the

82

door and set himself, took his deep breaths, and turned into the doorway.

It was a girl! She was wearing fatigues and a cap, but there was nothing else tough or warriorlike about her. Her eyes dropped from Leland to the automatic weapon on the table. She hesitated, then she lunged for it.

"Don't do it!"

She actually stopped—but then she looked up at him and went on, flinging herself onto the table and getting her hands on the weapon. Leland squeezed off a burst that hit her in the head and chest and blew her off the table and back against the wall.

He straightened up, his heart pounding. He couldn't delay. What was the attraction up here? He hurried around the table and into the next room. A safe—as simple as that. A big, deluxe, copper-colored wall job, now decorated with four small, shiny perfectly squared holes drilled around the wheel. Four kit bags were arrayed against the wall. He knew what he wanted, and it wasn't candy bars. The first two bags contained plastic explosive. He took three packets. The next bag had the detonating gear, including percussion caps. He threw that over his shoulder.

The elevator was coming. He hurried up the corridor and into the library, trying to keep track of the sound of the approaching car. With the explosive and the detonators, he had picked up another twenty pounds. He had just sworn off lifting. Being sick had taken something out of him. So had killing a girl. She had been twenty-three or four, a baby. *How'd you like it, boy? Now you've done it all!*

He stopped when he reached the corridor on the west side. Voices. He had to hang around. He was near the northwest stairs, having taken the one route he could depend on, and he was near the board room again. He had to gamble. He did not know how the offices were interconnected in this corner of the floor, or if doors were going to lock behind him, if he was not careful with them.

He passed through a luxury suite, working his way down to the typist's tiny quarters. Her door opened onto the broad hall leading down to the board room. With the door ajar, he could hear them plainly, speaking German, but he was too close—it was too dangerous.

He let the door close, and pressed his ear against it.

They were trying to get Karl to calm himself. The dead girl's name was Erika. They knew about Skeezix down on Wilshire Boulevard. Karl wanted to kill Leland himself. He didn't think they were going to accomplish their mission. Then Karl said something just beautiful: there were only nine of them left. Only? What was it that Stepin Fetchit used to say?

"Feets, do yo' stuff," Leland whispered.

First, he hid the detonators. If they caught him with them, they would be back on the track again. Even if they caught him without them, if he had been cute about his hiding place, they might figure it out. So the kit bag was in the wastepaper basket under the big desk in the suite's innermost office. The next step was in trying to get an idea of how they were going to search for him. He could have some influence on that: he could change the rules of the game.

He was on the thirty-sixth floor, going down, when he heard gunfire up above, loud and resonating. Somebody had had the bright idea that Leland would return to his redoubt in the elevator tower. No, it wasn't going to be that simple. He didn't have to be told twice that they were trying to guess his every move.

Hell, they had to, now.

And that was why he was not going down to the thirty-second floor to "surprise" them with another sortie. If Leland knew his man, Little Tony, Anton Gruber, word had already gone down on their secondary channel, and they were in the stairwells waiting for him.

Effectively, there were only seven. Two were downstairs, one in the basement, the other in the main lobby, where he had seen something fall out of Santa's sleigh onto Wilshire Boulevard. Leland wondered if anyone else had seen it. They might have been able to get the body out of view, but they weren't going to be able to hose down the steps.

Now Leland was having trouble holding onto the reasons why he had done it. To get attention. To show them they were dealing with someone who simply hadn't been lucky with Karl's brother. If they wanted to take him for a wild man, so much the better. He was having trouble holding on

84

and he knew it. He had never killed a girl before. Lucky Lindy, the last of the lonesome knights. What had made her think she could beat him? Skeezix's blood, that was it, which was now drying Leland's shirt to his skin. She had thought it Leland's blood, that he was terribly hurt. The next one won't be so easily fooled, Leland thought. It was not something he could count on anyway.

He stopped at the thirty-fourth floor, where the desks ranged in the open from one end of the building to the other. Of all the places he knew, this probably offered him the greatest real protection. The partitions on some of the other floors terrified him. With them, you were only out of sight, not out of danger. If he could use them to his own advantage, he would, but he couldn't figure out how.

More gunfire above. They were working their way down. They were conducting a sweep. Did they know how? Leland went to the elevator banks and pressed the call buttons. Nothing—no familiar whine. The elevators were closed down. Okay. No doubt about it, he was their top priority.

Probably the safest spot was in one of the corners. He selected the northeast, and began pushing desks together, trying to get as many thicknesses of sheet metal between him and them as he could. How many rounds had he left? Twelve in the Browning, a clip and a half for the Thompson, which could jam at any time. He had the plastic. If the packets were embedded with percussion cups, a burst of machine gun fire could set them off, and if he molded the packets over the red emergency lights over the stairwell doors, he would have a good chance of hitting them.

He glanced at his watch. 11:51. Nine minutes to Christmas. They were not interested in the Pope or anybody else outside the Klaxon building. Their business was on the fortieth floor. He thought of Steffie again. There was no reason for them to connect him with her. As long as he kept them busy, in fact, she was safe from them. Maybe.

He climbed over the desks to get into his improvised fortress. If he had it figured properly, there were far less than nine that he had to worry about—and another in the lobby. It would take at least two to guard the hostages. Five left. Now that Leland had the detonators, they could do nothing upstairs. So the maximum coming for him was five. If five people were searching for him, he didn't have a chance. Not like this. Not sitting here waiting for them.

But he couldn't see any other choice. They knew that he had gone into the ceiling panels to get over the partition on the fortieth floor. They were looking into anything that could hide a man, and judging by the gunfire, they were shooting at everything that looked questionable.

But with only five, it was impossible for them to watch all the stairwells while they searched the different floors. Still Leland hesitated. He wanted to make sure they met him on his terms. He did not want to get into a shootout in a stairwell with one of them when others could be only thirty or forty feet away.

Now he realized that if they had put five on the search for him, no one was left to even spot-check the stairwells on the thirty-second floor to keep him from escaping to all the floors below. Maybe they figured he wouldn't do that. What kind of connections were they making about him? And why were there so many of them? They wanted to get into the safe. They wanted to keep the hostages calm. They were here for the long haul. They had all the time they needed to find him.

11:56. He had let the girl get to him. The blood on his shirt had made her think he was hurt. Maybe the dirt on his face hadn't let her see his eyes. A nice looking kid. After the burst of .45-caliber bullets had hit her, she had looked as bad as Skeezix down on Wilshire.

He turned on the radio. Channel twenty-six.

"Are you there? Are you listening to me?"

Leland pressed the "Talk" button. He was looking out across Wilshire to the hills—in some places, faintly, he could see Christmas lights winking at random. "What have you got on your mind?"

"We are coming for you. We want our equipment. If you try to resist, we will start shooting hostages—"

"Don't crap me! You want to keep those people quiet!"

"No, no, you don't understand! We will bring them to you, wherever we find you, and shoot them there. Since you don't seem to mind killing women, we were thinking of a child—"

"Hang on, my other line is ringing." Leland turned the

radio off. He was watching a small crag in Laurel Canyon, trying to keep his eyes on it. There: one, two, three, four flashes of light. Dark again. He started counting. Nine seconds. One, two, three, four. He would have to climb out of here and go to the light switch near the stairwell if he wanted to return the signal. Four? What did four flashes mean? He climbed out. Now the interval was ten seconds. One, two, three, four. Okay, but what did it mean? He hurried. When he flicked the switch, the lights dazzled his eyes. Swell. He ran back to the window, trying to keep his eyes on the spot on the hill. Four flashes, a pause, four more, fast; then the light came on permanently and seemed to waver. It was three miles away. Somebody was swinging it in a circle. Four. Four flashes meant four, as in ten-four, because he had sent the signal by radio. Message understood.

He wept.

12:02.

"Merry Christmas," he whispered. He turned on the radio. "You still there? Sorry to keep you waiting. You've got more problems than just me. The other guy tells me that the cops are coming."

"I'm not surprised. We are prepared to be here for many days—weeks, if necessary."

Leland didn't answer. If it were true, why would he say so? Why, indeed. If they were prepared to last for weeks, the only problem they had, the one condition they couldn't control, was Leland himself. They knew exactly what they were doing, even to the talking on the radio. They had to consolidate their position. They wanted the detonators—and him dead—before the police began to understand the situation.

December 25

... 12:04 A.M., PST ...

THE WHOLE THING was a lot clearer to him now. He hadn't done that badly. He'd made a pest of himself and weakened their ranks and slowed them down. They'd expected a siege. The hostages were part of it. Something in that safe brought it all together. Some high-flying sharp-shooters in an oil company had just sold a bridge to the military junta in Chile—that was what he knew.

In itself that might be enough, but the old cop in Leland didn't like it. He felt like a cop again—in fact, wearing a badge wasn't a bad idea. If the place was going to be crawling with the LAPD, it might just save his life. He took the badge out of his wallet and turned the back into the light. THIS MAN IS A PRICK.

He put it on. At this point he'd rather have the hot coffee and doughnuts that always went with it.

He could use a cup of coffee. All the best police decisions were made over hot, bad coffee served in rough, earthenware mugs. If he slipped past them on the thirty-second floor, they would be permanently stymied, left to improvise the rest of the way. But the price was too high: he would lose his options with Steffie and the kids. The hostages would have to take their chances with whatever went down, as the guys out here liked to say, which he knew meant a SWAT assault—or worse, like the National Guard.

But if he stayed up above the thirty-second floor and they caught him, they would have the detonators and be back in business. Leland knew what they would do with him; he didn't need the questions of a taxi driver in St. Louis to remind him.

There was a third choice, although it involved some risk.

The way things were going, he would be more useful a bit further along, when the locals could make their presence felt. The only place to hide was one that had already been searched, and the only one not blocked by members of the gang was the thirty-second floor itself.

It was worth it. He might even be able to keep his eye on Steffie and the others. He had the radio—the only problem would be in locating a channel someone was monitoring.

Now there was more shooting—it sounded directly overhead. To hell with the plastic for now. He would remember where it was, as well as his little fortress in the corner.

On the thirty-third floor, he made his way through the maze of offices to Wilshire Boulevard. Empty. The traffic had been light-to-nonexistent five hours ago. He had been here that long. One puttering motorist would tell him that the area was still open.

Here came a prowl car, number one-four-nine, the numbers on the roof, visible from the air. A black-and-white, they called it out here. Doing fifteen miles an hour. Leland could almost make out the face of the officer driving. He was looking this way. He was looking very carefully, trying to appear unconcerned, a look Leland had seen on policemen around the world. He was looking at the steps. They were onto it—they were here. But it could be hours before they were here in force. It might be daylight before he knew anything more than he did now. When was daylight? Around seven. A solid seven hours away.

The elevators started, and it sounded like all of them at once. He had been told no lie: these people were prepared to deal with the police. This was the time to move, when their attention was directed elsewhere. He felt a frightening wave of exhaustion. If this was going to continue until dawn, he would have to find a place where he could hole up and sleep.

The bulbs in the stairwell lamps on the thirty-second floor had been removed. Leland held his breath—he could hear nothing but the whining of the elevators. They'd had something in mind for him, but it looked as if they had had to abandon it. Still, he went quietly, the kit bag tucked under his arm for silence, the Thompson ready. The stairwell was as black as the ventilator shaft. The elevators stopped—

again, seemingly all of them, and here, at the thirty-second floor. If he was going to find a place to hide, he had to do it now.

He knew exactly what was happening to him as soon as he felt the glass under his right foot, but his weight was pitched forward and he had generated too much momentum. His feet were gashed, the left worse than the right. The gang had been ready for him. He was motionless, holding on tightly to the banister, trying to keep from crying out.

The left foot had a big cut, a bad one. He had no one to blame but himself. They had taken the fluorescent tubes stacked in the stairway above the fortieth floor and broken them all over the stairwells. He should have known what they had in mind for him. Coming down from the roof, he had failed to notice that tubes had been moved. When he lifted his left foot back up to the step above his right, he could feel the blood pour off the ends of his toes. His instinct was to be careful, but he knew he had to hurry, even if they would be able to follow the trail he left to anyplace in the building. He had to get upstairs, but he had no idea of how he was going to tend to himself. The only first-aid equipment he knew of was in Stephanie's office. Bits of glass were embedded in his right foot; he could feel them grinding when he lifted his foot and set it down again.

He tried to go fast, but the cut in his left foot seemed to gush blood with every step. He hopped and skipped, trying to keep his weight off it, while the glass ground into the right foot. He went on up to the thirty-fourth floor, where at least he had the protection of his fortress.

Gunfire, just beyond the door. He stopped in the stairwell, his left foot raised above the rough concrete. It was running blood, the pain intensifying. Tomorrow he wouldn't be able to stand on either foot. He could feel the anger filling up in him again. He put both feet on the concrete, took his breaths, and pulled open the door.

The lights were on. The sound of the door opening made the girl in the middle of the room turn around, but she was too slow and startled by Leland's appearance, and a single short burst lifted her over the desk behind her.

Another automatic weapon went off, and the ceiling panels to Leland's left jumped and shattered. Leland had safety in the stairwell only if someone did not come upon him from above or below. He scrambled on his hands and knees across the floor to a position behind a desk. More fire, scattering items inches above his head. Leland knew where it was coming from, near his own fortress in the northeast corner. He moved to the next desk westward, poked his head up, and fired the Thompson as the other guy leaped over Leland's traffic jam of desks.

He was the only other one? Leland's feet were planted in puddles of blood. The lumps of plastic and detonators he had molded around the emergency lights were off to his right, not even in view. He moved over again, fired another burst at his fortress, and got down again. While the guy returned the fire, Leland got the last packet of plastic out of the kit bag and molded it around a detonator into a ball. In another moment, the guy was going to wake up, give his position on the radio, and call for help.

Leland worked his way around a little more. He'd killed four of them now, which wasn't bad, given the odds. This plastic was potent stuff, more than they needed for the safe, probably wrong for it, too. Now the guy was on the radio. Leland poked his head up and fired again, trying to penetrate his own defenses. He moved three or four desks closer to the northwest corner, until he could see the emergency lights to which he had molded the other packets. The other guy shot again, stitching the glass behind Leland. The cops downstairs were loving every minute of this. Cops everywhere liked to be in charge of the gunplay, and when guns were going off and they weren't in on it, it made them more than a little bit crazy.

"Hey, creep! Do you speak English?"

"Yes I do, you human filth!"

"Take a good look at those emergency lights by the elevators!"

He laughed. "I saw that movie, *Sergeant York!* Gary Cooper made a birdcall!"

Leland hadn't had that in mind; but then he remembered that the old man downstairs had made him think of *Sergeant York*—now what filled his thoughts was what these people had probably done to that old man.

"Look again, dummy!"

Leland saw his head coming up. "Wait!" he shouted. "Don't shoot at it!"

Leland had the Thompson trained on him. The first rounds hit the guy in the neck and high in the chest, driving him back and passing through him to shatter the window beyond. Leland stood up and emptied the clip into him, keeping him upright and driving him back against the glass and then through it, three hundred and forty feet above the ground. Leland glanced again at the plastic on the emergency lights. He'd thought he knew what it was. It had certainly scared hell out of Skeezix's new friend. Later—first, Leland had to tend to his feet. No, first he had to figure out how.

On his way out, he discarded the Thompson and picked up the girl's machine gun—a Kalashnikov at last—and three full clips of ammunition.

He went down to the thirty-third floor, looking for an office similar to his daughter's, hoping to find something besides paper, towels, and toilet tissue. He could walk, but walking made him bleed. He was on the south side of the building, on the assumption that the gang would have its attention turned to Wilshire Boulevard, where the black-and-white had been spotted.

He picked the last of the glass out of his right foot, then studied the left. The gash was in the pad behind the smallest two toes, a good three-eighths of an inch deep, jagged, almost an inch and a half long. It had been a long time since he had seen his own meat like this. If it could be treated properly, the cut would give him no problems. But he didn't know if he would even find something to tie around it temporarily. Finally he remembered that the best offices had the corner views.

He found a Turkish hand towel, and he folded it once lengthwise and then tried to tie it, but it wasn't long enough. His temper started to flare again. He wanted to kill them all? Now it crossed his mind that he was glad he still had most of them left.

He caught himself. First he had to bind his foot. He sat up—where the hell was he, anyway? This was a business office. He hopped across the room to the desk and got a handful of rubber bands. Good. In fact, it was pretty slick. The thickness of the towel cushioned the pressure of the rubber bands.

He wanted to see what was playing on the radio. Twenty-six was quiet. He dialed to nine.

"Come in," a voice whispered. It was a young, black voice, deep, with no trace of ghetto. "If the person who radioed for help can hear me, acknowledge this transmission if you can."

Leland pressed the "Talk" button. "You got him. Listen: you've got seven foreign nationals armed with automatic weapons and high explosive, perhaps a lot more, holding approximately seventy-five civilians hostage on the thirty-second floor. They've killed one. He's on the fortieth floor. In addition to the two birds who took the short way down, I've killed three others, including two women—"

There was a pause. "You want to identify yourself, fella?"

"Not possible. If I get the chance, I'll throw my wallet out to you."

"What else can you tell us?"

"The leader of the gang is a German named Anton Gruber, a.k.a. Antonino Rojas, Little Tony the Red, with a call on him in the German Federal Republic. He has enough explosive in here to flatten the place, which may be what he has in mind if he doesn't get what he wants, whatever that is. On the other hand, I've got the detonators, or at least some of them—"

"Throw them out."

"Can't right now, and I don't think it's a good move. As long as he thinks he can get me and make me tell him where the detonators are, he won't play his last card, the hostages."

"You talk like a man who knows something, if you understand me. I want you to throw the detonators out. The first objective is to reduce the chance of disaster."

"I already have, until they catch me. Let me talk. From what I can tell, they have the elevators locked up on the thirty-second floor. You try to shoot your way in, from above or below, and they're going to start killing women and children. Call your boss and ask him if he wants children shot on Christmas in his town."

"I want you to listen to me—"

"*No*, you listen: I'm wounded and I left a trail of blood to where I am now. They're still after me. I won't be leaving a trail anymore; let me protect myself and I'll get back to you."

Leland turned the radio off. He had been in one place long enough. He had to get himself together and understand how the situation had changed. He wanted to talk some more with the police.

He was limping, but he could move. It was like walking on loaves of bread. His left foot felt as though it had been sliced in half. He would know if he started bleeding badly again. He went upstairs, taking the southeast staircase, hurrying the first flight to get past the thirty-fourth floor, then slowing and feeling the pain the next two. Good enough. He was tired anyway. He wanted to rest.

Of all the aircraft he'd owned after the war, the best had been his Cessna 310. During the war he had flown all sorts of things, of course, from training planes up through the Thunderbolt, a heavy-handling, evil-looking brute, to the Mustang, the best single-engine piston aircraft ever built, bar none. He had been happiest thinking about airplanes and flying. On the day he'd checked out in the 310, he'd dropped the salesman off at the office and taxied back out to the runway again. The kid in the tower had told him to keep the wings on—he'd known how good Leland was feeling that day. . . .

The thirty-sixth floor was like the thirty-third, a gridiron of tiny cubicles surrounded by equally tiny, but color-coordinated offices—in a big corporation, you always knew where you stood in relation to the top.

It had no status now, with bulletholes, splintered panels, and broken glass everywhere. He was on the north side again, sitting on the floor behind a desk, looking down into Wilshire Boulevard. Three blocks away, he could see the flash of a boiling light against a building. A helicopter appeared over the hills, then swung around abruptly and headed north, toward the San Fernando valley.

Leland was eating his Milky Way. He'd finished the Oh Henry!, and he was saving the Mars bar for last. He felt like a kid in the movies, or a young cop eating for energy in a prowl car. . . .

He'd taken the 310 straight out to sea at a height of a thousand feet, across the New Jersey suburban blight where every tacky, upright swimming pool stood revealed, every van, every bolt-together aluminum tool shed—at a thousand feet, at one hundred and fifty miles an hour, the suburbs looked like an enormous junkyard.

But then he'd gone on, out over the ocean. Two miles out, he was at five hundred feet; ten miles, fifty feet. By then he was making better than two hundred knots, faster than he'd flown in almost twenty years. It was a brilliant, blue-sky day, with only a few cirrus clouds far above. The sun was over his shoulder and the water looked very dark, so close the waves seemed to be nipping at the plane. He passed a sport fishing boat and waggled his wings. The 310 was his second twin, with wingtip fuel tanks, as pretty as any general aviation aircraft ever, loaded, equipped for IFR, one of the first small radars—he had world-wide capability.

At thirty miles out, he came upon two freighters, five miles apart, making for the Ambrose Light. Using their superstructures as pylons, he flew figure eights; and when the crews came out on deck, he waggled his wings, climbed straight up, rolled, stalled, let it fall, and finished with a full loop between the ships where both crews could see. When he headed back to the land, he could see arms waving from the decks. . . .

He pressed the "Talk" button. "You guys still there?"

"Ah, how you doing? What happened to you?"

"I had to get the show on the road. For the last ten, I've been cooping."

"Right. A couple of us heard your earlier transmission, and we agree that you're the real thing. We're going to take a chance on you. Now how do you make the situation?"

"The roof is easier to defend than to take. They're very heavily armed—"

"How about you?"

Leland thought of the Browning, and that Little Tony might be listening. "I'm in business," he said.

98

"How do we recognize you?"

Leland smiled. "I'm black. I wasn't when I started, but I am now."

"I hear you. We'll talk about that later. What about the radio? How did you come into that?"

No wonder: they hadn't figured out that he had one of the gang's radios.

"I came into this the same way I came into this sweet little Kalashnikov machine gun. It's logical to assume they're tuned in, too. Do you know who Little Tony is?"

"Hey, I usually work out of Hollenbeck, I was on my way home to West L.A."

"Okay," Leland said. "He's third generation Red Army Faction, West Germany. After Andres Baader died, his people went deep underground. Nobody knew where they would turn up, but the stories were always that they would do something big. Here we are." Leland had a sudden thought: what if the marshal on the plane from St. Louis had been responding to some wild, incoherent information? If Leland had been paying attention and identified himself, he might have learned something that could have prevented this.

"How do you know all this stuff?"

"Just say it's a long time since I worked Hollenbeck. Look, I told you: these guys need me, and it's not a good idea to stay on the air too long."

"Well, we're going to give them a taste now."

Leland froze. The police still did not understand the situation. He had become convinced that Little Tony was listening. Leland moved closer to the window—and now, faintly, he heard one of the elevators running. He couldn't be sure that they weren't coming for him. No, such a short trip would have been completed already.

They had been listening! They were headed down to meet the police!

Leland pressed the "Talk" button. "Our conversation was monitored. They're coming to meet you."

"Right on," the black voice said. "Thanks a lot."

With only seven of them left, Leland didn't think they would mount another mission against him. He got up—he needed a cane, or even crutches. He made his way from one doorway to the next. If he was going to continue to be effective, he would have to figure some way to make the gang come to him. There was no point in staying at the window. If there was to be a firefight down in the street, this was the best place to get hurt. He had an idea, anyway. And a thought to bear in mind later: on the basis of the information he had given them, police snipers could assume they could shoot at any target above the thirty-second floor.

He had to give an account of himself, or the gang would know how badly he was hurt. If they sent someone after him while he was exposed and vulnerable, that would be the end, surely. But he knew he would be better off in the long run if he could keep them thinking that with him they still had more than they could handle.

He needed a chair on casters, an electric typewriter, and a fireax. The floor was quiet. His bleeding had stopped, but the pain was intensifying. He remolded his ball of plastic explosive until it was the shape of a football, with the detonator in the middle. He put it on the seat of the chair. Carefully he put the electric typewriter on top of the explosive, tied the typewriter to the chair with its cord, then pushed the chair toward the elevator banks.

Now he heard popping of gunfire out on the street. The position of the elevator banks on the lobby floor and the locations of the garage entrances below that, limited the terrorists' field of fire in all directions on the street level, but from above, three or four stories up, they could keep the police from ever getting near the building.

The gang would be ready for armored cars. There were iron gates across the garage entrances, and an armored car with wounded men in it stalled at the bottom of the ramp would be impassable. This wasn't wartime, when the order would be given to blow it away. Policemen did not kill brother officers in the line of duty. It was more than society had a right to ask.

He could hear gunfire coming up the elevator shaft. What he was waiting for was the sound of a car in motion. He would not have a lot of time, and there was nothing he could do in advance, for it involved using the fireax on the door. As soon as it was heard and understood on the thirty-second

100

floor, they would be after him. He heard automatic rifle fire from outside.

He got out the radio. "How are you guys doing?"

"Well, I guess you were telling us the truth. Some people thought you were a psycho. They're kicking the shit out of us. You say there were twelve?"

"Now seven."

"Well, you're one tough fucking dude, let me tell you."

"Stay tuned." Leland said, and put the radio away. One of the elevators was in motion. He wheeled the chair into position, then turned to the elevator door with the ax. With the first swing, the pain in his left foot was so severe that he nearly dropped the ax on it. The next swing got the blade of the ax into the crack of the door and broke something inside, because the door opened, then was forced shut again. He rotated the handle of the ax so that the door came open again, enough for him to get his hand in and pull it open wide, and block it open with the length of the ax handle.

He looked in—and bullets hit the top of the door. The car, coming up, was still a long way down. Leland had to return the fire—he had to show he was still fit. He poked the Kalashnikov into the shaft and fired a burst down toward the car on the thirty-second floor from which the firing had come. Far below, someone in the ascending car fired at him, the round pinging upward toward the roof. Leland got behind the chair and rolled it like a baby carriage into the shaft. If the guy saw the thing coming down, he might think it was Leland. Even if it didn't go off, his chair-bomb would go through the roof of the car.

Suddenly the shaft filled with brilliant light, and in the fraction of a second before he heard the sound, Leland knew he had accomplished far more than he had intended. The roar was the loudest sound he had ever heard in his life, and the concussion wave flung him through the air across the corridor and against the elevator door on the other side. He never lost consciousness, and he could feel the building continuing to shake as he slid to the bottom of the door. The floor was bouncing like a high school gymnasium during a dance. He could feel the building yawing. It wasn't his imagination—downstairs, people were screaming.

101

Then the motion was gone, but it had lasted long enough for him to understand what he had done. He had to get moving before he could start broadcasting again. The blast had knocked the wind out of him. Everyone else, too, he hoped.

HE HAD TO go up. The shooting had stopped. What the hell, he'd put the fear of God into everybody, including himself. Climbing stairs was laborious and very painful now; for a while he found it easier to go backwards, but he could feel his muscles knotting. That was exhaustion, too. He went on past the thirty-seventh floor. The only thing that could genuinely surprise them at this point was more effort than they thought he was capable of exerting. He could see that his mood had changed, that he had found another way of keeping himself pumped up. He didn't think anyone was in any immediate danger because of the damage he had done to the building. The weight of the people involved was nothing compared to the weight of the structure itself. He was having trouble remembering what he was doing and what he was doing it for. Killing the second girl had been easier than killing the first. Nagasaki and Hiroshima—nobody remembered Nagasaki. He'd had enough killing. He was sick of it.

He got out on the thirty-ninth floor, the computer installation. The floor was sealed off from even the daylight, great banks of electronic hardware bathed in their own dull gray emergency lighting. Curiously, none of the equipment had been damaged. Either the terrorists were as in awe of it as everybody else, or they planned to use it themselves in their journey into madness they thought was revolution.

Leland had seen the sheet on Anton Gruber a half dozen times. "Little Tony the Red" was supposed to lend him a certain glamor. He was thirty years old, the son of a Stuttgart industrialist, raised by nurses, sent to private schools. On his eighteenth birthday he was given a Mercedes; on his nineteenth, another. Through the late sixties, he ran with a bunch of indolent rich kids who open their summers at Saint-Tropez, winters at Gstaad. Some of those people had been on the arty fringe of the Baader-Meinhof gang, and gradually Anton Gruber was drawn in. He denounced his parents and accused his father of the "crimes" of hypocrisy, complacency, and arrogance.

There was more to it than that: Gruber *père* had been an officer in the S.S. during the war, like so many presently successful German businessmen. Automobiles, electronics—the old Nazis were everywhere, silent about the past, smug about the present. A generation of the damned, whose children hated their parents' lies and self-justifications. It was not all that different in America. Steffie had suffered in her life most of all at the hands of her parents, when they had been insisting insanely that their marriage was still alive.

Rivers was probably Gruber's sixth or seventh victim. Dr. Hanns Martin Schleyer, an industrialist like Gruber's father, had been executed the same way, a bullet through the lapel. Leland had heard that the West German police had taps of Gruber gloating that he made sure his victims were dressed properly when he pinned the black boutonniere. Anton Gruber was fascinated by death, the presence and the look of it.

He was not the only one among them like that, either. Some of it was poetic German horseshit, but Ursula Schmidt, in an essay expressing her "final commitment to violence," wrote of her "womb of death to which men return for eternal rest."

Leland might have just killed her.

He didn't know who he had killed anymore: a generation ago, their fathers, uncles', possibly their mothers. In this building was a man who had just lost his brother because of Leland, unless Leland had just killed him, too.

The offices up here had clear glass half-walls facing the equipment itself, part of the paranoia that surrounded computers. The highest priests had to keep the totems in sight. He could not help grinning at the reaction tomorrow of the computer's attendants to the filth he was dragging in here. He wanted to take a position near the windows on Wilshire, although it would give him no protection. Perhaps that

104

would work for him: given his past performance, they might not think he would be so stupid. He shook his head—that kind of thinking would get him killed.

Even from this height, the results of the terrorists' preparation for battle could be seen. A black-and-white piled up against a lamp pole, the driver lying face down just outside the door. Leland looked up. Two hundred feet above the building, beginning to dissipate, was a great, gray cloud. Sure, the blast had been heard all over the basin: there were ten times as many lights on around the city as there had been a few minutes ago. It made Leland realize something else. He stretched out behind a desk and switched on the radio.

"What do you think a building like this costs?"

"Hey, twelve million. Twenty—who knows? How are you doing?"

"I knocked myself on my can. That was one packet of their explosive. I've got two more. Be careful of what you say, because they're monitoring us."

"I understand that now."

"Don't sweat it. Is the building on fire?"

"Not so we can see. Now we want to know what happened."

Leland told him. "I saw one in the elevator. They have the escape hatches pulled because of a number I did on them earlier. So now we're down to six."

"We had a report from one of our people that he saw two of them back into the elevator. They have some kind of a barricade on the ground floor."

"Well, I saw one. You have to figure six left. I can't count probables here. Now tell me about the building."

"The seventeenth and eighteenth floors are completely blown out, and you have windows smashed all the way up and down the building. They're going to have tear the sucker down."

"Was anybody hurt?"

"Not by you. We have two men hit. You blew crap all over the neighborhood. That explosive is strong medicine. I saw a desk and chair go sailing clear over Wilshire Boulevard. Hold on. Don't go away."

While he waited, Leland looked for evidence of the damage he had done. A hole the size of a compact car was drilled through a cigarette billboard, and across the street, the front of the squat, little building looked like the victim of a riot.

"Hey, boss, you still there?"

"Merry Christmas," Leland said.

"Merry Christmas to you. I'm going to turn the radio over to my commanding officer, Captain Dwayne T. Robinson, okay?"

He sounded like he was introducing a guest speaker. "Okay," Leland laughed.

"This is Dwayne Robinson. How are you?"

"Fine."

"No, *who* are you? I want to know your name."

"I can't tell you that right now."

"Why not?"

"Next question."

"You've given us some information here. How did you come by it? Why are you in that building?"

Leland stayed silent. The guy wanted to control the situation from outside, if he could—*if:* old Dwayne T. wasn't thinking clearly.

"Are you still there?"

"Yeah. Put the other guy back on."

"No, I'm giving the orders here. We don't need any more of your kind of cooperation. I want you to lay down your weapons and retreat to a safe location. That explosion did a tremendous amount of property damage and threatened the lives of scores of people. Now these are the lawful orders of a policeman, and you are liable to arrest and penalties if you refuse to obey them."

"Put the other guy on," Leland said. "I don't want to talk to you any more."

"Now, listen, fuckhead—!"

"No!" Leland screamed. "You listen to me! You've got six psychos holding seventy-five people at gunpoint. They have enough high explosive to flatten this end of the city. What they don't have is the means to detonate it, because of me. They're down to half their strength, because of me. As long as I'm in business, they can't get themselves set up the way they would like. Do you think you can stop them down there? Come on, tell me—you're the fuckhead! If you think

106

I'm going to put up with your shit now and not have your chief kick your ass all the way down to Terminal Island when it's done, *you don't know me!* Put the other guy on! *Now!*"

Silence.

"Here you go," the black man said. "How're you feeling?"

"Like I should have saved my strength. Who *is* that turdlet?"

"Don't draw me into that kind of talk. I can understand that you're tired and under strain, but down here it seemed like you were overreacting just a little, if you know what I mean."

There was something comforting about common sense coming from someone decades his junior, Leland decided. "I'm sorry. At this point, this kind of fighting looks easier than that kind of fighting."

"I hear you, partner. Just kick back and relax a while, hear?"

"It's been a long time since I've been called partner. Are you on the street?"

"No, I'm inside."

"All the years I was a cop, I was always on the street."

"How old are you?"

"Old enough to be your father."

He laughed. "Not *mine!*"

"I said, you oughta get a look at me now. What detail do you have at Hollenbeck?"

"Juvenile. We have a whole big show there."

"You like kids?"

"I love kids. Say, man, is there someone we can reach out for via the land line who can identify you? Once we establish your credibility, we can get going on who these people are."

"It's the long way around, but I see what you mean. You call William Gibbs, in Eureka, California. Tell him what's happening and where, and the first two words out of his mouth will be my name."

"Gotcha. Anybody else?"

"A Ms.—got that? *Mz?*—Kathi Logan." Leland gave him the area code and her number. "Tell her I was wishing her a Merry Christmas when I was cut off. She'll understand."

"I'll do that exactly right. Don't you worry about it. Why don't you get some rest?"

"No, I'm going to tune in on the opposition a while."

"You do that?"

"Channel twenty-six. Don't let them kid you. They all speak English."

"We heard the German, but none of us can handle it. We're getting it on tape. What have they been telling you?"

"Little Tony likes to think he's a seductive, persuasive guy. You've already heard everything I've been able to figure out. Nothing so complicated: he juices my fruit, and I juice his."

More laughter. "I'm going to tune in."

"What the hell—people are dying left and right, but it's all in fun, right?"

"If you say so."

Leland dialed to channel twenty-six. "Are you there, Tony?"

"Yes, Mr. Leland. It took me a moment to adjust my receiver. Mr. Leland, are you listening?"

Yes. "Yes." He almost didn't say it aloud.

"We have here your colleague, Mr. Ellis."

Leland closed his eyes. "How are you, Ellis?"

"All right, Joe." It was a voice on the edge of terror. Leland couldn't remember Ellis's first name. "Listen to me," he said, echoing Leland's words to Dwayne T. Robinson, Lieutenant, LAPD—*listen to me:* some kind of Mayday into the void: "Listen: they want you to tell them where the detonators are. They know people are listening. They want the detonators, or they're going to kill me, Joe. Joe, I've done you a lot of favors in the recent past. I want you to think of that. I thought you would understand that, Joe. Joe, are you listening?"

Favors? He was telling Leland that he was shielding Steffie, but was favors the word he thought expressed what he was doing? If Leland didn't turn over the detonators, would he tell them who Stephanie was, to keep himself alive? "Yeah, I hear you."

"Tell them where the detonators are. The police are here. It's their problem now."

"I can't tell them. I'd have to show them. Then what? What happens to me?"

"Mr. Leland." It was Little Tony. "What Mr. Ellis has hesitated to tell you is that we are going to kill him straightaway if you do not yield our equipment at once."

"There are people here, Joe," Ellis said. He meant Steffie. He'd already said that he hadn't identified her. What was he threatening? Leland closed his eyes. *Goodbye, Ellis*.

"I don't believe them," Leland said into the radio. *God forgive me*, he thought.

Through the little radio speaker, the shot sounded like a rush of air, and the screams that followed seemed very far away.

Leland pressed the "Talk" button. "All right. I'll give you what you want."

"We want the detonators," said Little Tony.

"Let me get them and put them where you can find them."

"Excellent. And where will that be?"

"Uh-uh. I'll drop them off first and get clear, then I'll call you."

"You have five minutes."

"I need more time," Leland said. "I've got a long way to go and I'm no longer in the best of shape."

"Ten."

"I can't do it. Not that fast."

A pause; then: "How long will it take you?"

"Twenty minutes, maybe half an hour."

"Twenty minutes, then we will shoot someone else, perhaps this time a woman." There was silence. Leland pressed the "Talk" button.

"You guys get all that?"

"Meet us on channel nine," the black officer said flatly.

"Now I know they can hear me, but I want to find out what the fuck you think you're doing up there." It was Dwayne Robinson. "First you tell us that you don't want to give your name, then that punk calls you Leland—is that your name?"

"Yeah. Billy Gibbs will give you the rest of the information."

"We've got somebody talking to him. Why all the bullshit? I want an explanation—now."

Leland stayed silent. Anything he could say would let Little Tony figure it out.

"Now listen to me, you son of a bitch," Robinson snarled. "Everything that went down between you and that punk is on tape down here. You let that man die. I don't give a fuck who your friends are, if there's a way to jam your ass in jail, I'm going to do it."

"Go fuck yourself," Leland said. He turned the radio off.

This was going to kill him, he knew. He did not know what to do but go out and meet them head-on. He was trying to remember that there was no sense in being stupid about it. He hobbled to the southwest staircase, trying to decide if he should go upstairs and fight it out with whoever was there. If he won, he could hold the position.

What time was it? Almost three o'clock, deep into the black hours before dawn, when people died anyway. He didn't want to die. He wasn't ready to die. He wanted a bath first. They hosed you down at the morgue, but an undertaker would clean his head and hands and bury the rest of him dirty.

He did not want to die while Steffie and the children were in this danger. That was why he was on this rampage. He didn't start the killing. Rivers died first. And how bad a job was he doing? He'd bagged five of them before the cops had even arrived. If he had it to do over, he would do it exactly the same way. Goddamn, he couldn't imagine how he could have done it any *other* way.

He knew he was exhausted. "Man, you are beat," he said aloud. He had been awake twenty-two hours, and he knew from experience that the worst was to come—but that with the daylight he would be good for another full day. The body was habituated to sleep, but could easily do without it for one night. He had to manage himself carefully for the next three or four hours, if he lived that long.

He stopped at the elevator banks. If the blast had blown out two floors, the chair must have hit the roof of the car when it was between, or nearly between, them. Leland was wondering what had been done to the east bank. The doors on both floors would have been blown away, but the cars—

110

and more importantly, the cables—had been above the explosion. As long as you stayed above, say, the twentieth floor, just to play it safe, then everything should work perfectly. Naturally, the gang would hear the electric motor humming, unless some other noise masked it.

All right, he knew something. What did he do with it?

It was as if he had been reduced to functioning with only shreds of himself, he felt so drained. He had to make so many new, strange connections to hold himself together.

He switched the radio on. "Tony. Tony, are you there?"

"It is a matter of more than passing curiosity to me, Mr. Leland, how you happen to know my name—and so much about us."

"You just happened to run into exactly the wrong guy." Leland knew it was a mistake as soon as it was out of his mouth: it contained no hint of the capitulation implicit in turning over the detonators. Silence. It was as if Leland could hear the bastard's wheels grinding.

"Tell me, Mr. Leland, why were you so interested in concealing your name from us?"

"I know so much about you that I couldn't be sure that you didn't know something about me."

"What difference would that have made?"

"You would have taken me a lot more seriously than you have."

"Yes, that's true. Very good. You're a wily opponent—"

"Look, I only called to tell you that I'm doing what I said."

"I know," the voice purred. "The reception is of a different quality, and I have to point the antenna in a different direction."

You son of a bitch. Leland was thinking of the kid who was giving his father the big screen television set. How did he know that story? Yes, the chauffeur. Asleep in his bed, bless him. Unless he had been awakened by the explosion. "Why did you kill Ellis?"

"Why did you let him die?"

Leland was moving toward the stairs again, thinking that it was what Gruber wanted: only in the stairwells did they have a chance of hearing Leland's voice—and not on the radio, either. "That won't wash, Tony. I saw you kill Rivers.

You had no reason to do that. You wanted him to open the safe, but you were prepared to do it youself. You killed him because you felt like killing somebody, but you did it on the fortieth floor, where the hostages wouldn't see it. All evening you've been trying to keep them calm, and now suddenly you've changed your act."

"Well, that was your doing, Mr. Leland. Surely you understand that. The explosion set off a panic down here. You seem to be such a warrior, you must know that you left us with no choice but to show them that we have the capacity to realize our aims."

Leland was in the stairwell. "You really know how to lay it on, Tony. The people you had to convince were your own. You're not doing so well, kid. Karl wants action, doesn't he? You made a mistake. You let Karl pressure you. When you have to start showing people how tough you are, you're already finished. You're a walking corpse, Tony. Start getting used to the idea of being dead."

"Like to have a word with you, Mr. Leland." It was Hollenbeck, with his nice, easy way of talking.

"I planned to go off the air."

"Good plan. We're picking up an awful lot of traffic in German on channel thirty—"

Leland switched off and went back up the stairs.

headed down the hall, he heard a girl giggling behind him. He stopped.

"Drop the gun, please."

He did.

"Now turn around."

It was a little blonde girl in fatigues too big for her, holding an automatic with both hands. Her eyes widened when she saw the badge. "You are a policeman? Where are the detonators? Quick, tell me."

"On the roof."

"Ah, yes, I see. With two fingers only, please, remove the pistol."

He held it out for her. She dropped it in her kit bag. "Now tell me where on the roof."

"You have to go around to the right. There's a staircase up to the elevator tower and an aluminum box opposite—"

She waggled the revolver. "Show me."

He opened the door. She stayed behind him as they went up the stairs. All but a few of the fluorescent bulbs were gone. Mistake number one. He didn't know what the hell he was going to do when they got to Skeezix's gun. She was being too careful. He wasn't going to get anywhere near it.

"This is really too bad," she said. "You seemed to enjoy killing so much. But you are really only a trained dog. You destroy the building in order to save it."

"Honey, I don't give a flying fuck about the building." He was at the top of the stairs. "I have to open the door."

"Just a moment." He heard the click of her radio switch. She spoke at some length in German. Little Tony answered and then she said, "Nein, nein," like a woman telling a man she didn't need his help. Leland was beginning to think of something else.

"Now open the door," she said.

The wind was stronger than ever, a warm, roiling gale out of the hills. The sky was clear in all directions.

"You didn't ask me why I didn't care about the building."

"Are you trying to tell me something, old man? Go on, keep moving."

"You people aren't thinking. Why didn't I just work my way down and out of the building?"

"I want to hear this. I want you to tell me everything.

115

Now, with nothing remaining, you want to justify yourself."

"The detonators are on the other side of that box, Ursula."

"What? That's not my name—" He threw himself at her, and she shot him, once, in the left thigh. But then he was falling on her, and when the gun discharged the second time, the muzzle blast scalded his arm. She was falling, with nothing to absorb the shock. He was afraid that the gun would go off again, and he rolled to the left, away. He punched her in the face, but she tried to get the gun around, and he punched her again. She got his thumb in her mouth and bit down hard. She was trying to knee him in the groin. He grabbed her hair with his other hand and slammed her head down on the roof. She opened her mouth. He punched her again. His leg wasn't broken, thank God. He punched her three more times, and when the fight was out of her, he twisted the gun from her hand and go to his feet and shot her in the right eye. He was shaking with rage and relief and the exultation of victory. He pulled the trigger again. When the gun was empty he pulled the trigger three more times, and the last thing to pass through his mind was the notion of throwing her body off the roof, too, just to let Tony know he still had his store open, And then Leland fainted.

He didn't know how long he had been out, and the time on his watch, 3:38, wasn't much help. The bullet wound was in the flesh on the outside of his thigh, two small holes five inches apart, the exit wound almost as neat as the entry. A patch of blood the size of a pie plate glistened in the reflective light. He crawled behind the aluminum box and set up Skeezix's gun. He had the strap of his kit bag for a tourniquet, but he didn't think he would need it. More gunfire from the street.

Maybe he had been out less than a minute. This time he wasn't going to announce his continued presence. He had another thought: these people weren't getting tired. In addition to their own amphetamines, maybe they had found Ellis's cocaine, too. Assholes—they deserved each other. He had a clear view of the staircase door as well as the door leading into the elevator tower. He watched both. No surprises.

"Hannah?" someone called.

The man was coming up the stairs. He could have been close enough to hear the shots. This one would be number eight. The door was hinged to swing Leland's way.

"Hannah?"

The door started to open. Leland got down low.

"Hannah?"

The door was wide open, but no one appeared. The door started to close again, and Leland fired, slamming the door shut. He waited.

"We're going to leave you up here for now," Little Tony called. "But don't worry, we'll be back in the daylight, and then we will kill you. I will kill you myself—believe me, it will be better that way."

There was another long burst of automatic rifle fire from the street.

"Hey, Hollenbeck."

"Hey, my man! How are ya?"

"I'm on the roof. I think they've locked the door. I took one in the leg, but it's no big thing. Oh, yeah, scratch one more."

"You're kidding me!"

"She's lying right here beside me. Name of Hannah."

"Ah, shit."

"This is the third woman. I'm almost getting used to it. What's going on down there?"

"Our German ace showed up and he's been giving us their play-by-play. We've got so many radios going down here that I didn't hear anything about women. That's really disgusting."

"Stop being old-fashioned."

"He told us that they were after you, and Robinson tried to get a diversion going. Two things: are you sure about the total number? We are very definitely on hold down here."

"It's what I heard them say. What made Robinson see the light?"

"Well, now we know who you are, man! He's still cursing you out, but at least he knows—we all do—that he's dealing with somebody who knows what he's doing. That's the

117

second question. The German ace picked up something about you wearing a badge. What's that about?"

"It's just something I had. I put it on so you'll know me when I walk out of here."

"Well, that's what they're for. You go on wearing it. Now we got a deputy chief on the site, fully briefed and in charge. Billy Gibbs says he wishes he was covering you, by the way. Hang on." He had the "Talk" button still depressed, for Leland heard him say, "He got another one. That's seven."

"Son of a bitch." The radio went dead a moment. "Joe? Vince Crane here. We met two years ago in New Orleans."

"How are ya?" He'd been in New Orleans two years ago, but he couldn't place Crane in the huge Los Angeles delegation at that conference.

"I'm okay. I think we're going to be okay with this, thanks to you. I wouldn't want to face twelve of them. Now listen, for now, we think it a good idea to let them speak their piece. We want you to hold tight, if you can. We understand the problem, and we're taking all due care, believe me. Are you going to be all right?"

"When you send out for food, put me down for coffee and a jelly doughnut."

He laughed. "Well, you take it easy for a while. I'll give you back to Sergeant Powell."

"Hey, partner," Leland said.

"That's right, and I'm honored. You have the scam now, don't you? More news for you. I was talking with Kathi Logan. She doesn't remember you *at all!*"

"I'll get you for that, fella."

"No, she said a whole lot of nice things about you, man. All she knows is that you're stuck in a building with some bad people. Now something else: the media are showing up and that's in a big way. They want to patch the two of you in, when they can. You lose your privacy, but it's something."

"I don't want a circus."

"It's a little late for that, *kimosabe.*"

"I'll catch you later, Hollenbeck."

"Call me Al."

"Joe. Later."

"You bet. Take care now."

118

... 4:53 A.M., PST ...

PAIN AWAKENED HIM. He knew where he was before he opened his eyes, but it took another moment before he remembered it all, or his memory caught up with the rest of him. He wasn't even sure he could move, he was hurting so badly in so many places. Even his thumb was cut, where Hannah had bitten him. The temperature had dropped or, more likely under the circumstances, his resistance had lowered just that much. Before he had fallen asleep, he had figured he had lost about a pint of blood, or the amount you gave at the blood bank, which was a hell of a lot of blood to lose. The sky was still black. At this time of year, there would be another hour and a half of total darkness.

He wanted to try standing up again. He had walked here, to the spot on the Wilshire Boulevard side where he had squeezed out of the ventilator. His left foot was so bad that he wanted to cry out. His thigh burned. He had been grazed by a bullet in his youth, and it had felt the same. He could walk, but he could see it was going to take five minutes to get around to the other side of the roof where Hannah's body lay. He stopped—why the hell did he want to go there? He was going to have to calculate every step. He got out the radio, but he waited a moment before he turned it on.

Something was bothering him. Al—Hollenbeck—had asked him about the number in the gang. Why? Leland had heard the same gunfire. These kids had studied this stuff in guerilla camps throughout the Middle East. They could set up a field of fire as well as the U.S. Marines. Al might not know that; his work kept him occupied around the clock.

Leland had decided that he was only going to listen.

Twenty-six was quiet. On nineteen, a woman was speaking German, reciting words and numbers. Nothing on nine. The police had their own frequencies, but that did not mean that the gang could not listen to them, too, with the right equipment.

He was going to have to get ready for them. It would be more than an hour before they came for him. They would want to wait until the sun was up over the mountains. The worst of it for him was not knowing about Stephanie. He did not want to outlive her. He hadn't wanted to outlive Karen, either. He did not want to go through that grief again. He didn't think he could.

He shook his head. People were coming to kill him in an hour, and he was worrying about living too long. He made his way to the edge of the roof, but his leg made it impossible for him to get up on the sign to look down onto Wilshire Boulevard. He was wondering again about the wisdom of not getting on the air. The police could have something to tell him.

It seemed that there were many, many more lights on all around the city. He'd bought the 310 after the divorce. He'd known it was going to be his last plane, and toward the end he didn't even use it much. There was a time in your life to quit certain things. For the past six or seven years he'd devoted himself almost completely to his work. Good, interesting work, too.

He had been on the team that had devised the first antiterrorist, antikidnapping driving course. He'd designed the security system in the first of the new ball parks, and it had been copied, or adhered to, ever since. And something he had learned not to tell people, that he'd been the one to advise the national retailers to force manufacturers of small items like ballpoint pens to mount them on cards too big for people to slip into their pockets. People hated having to gouge their way through the cardboard and plastic so much that it did no good to tell them that it had to be done because shoplifting the world over was so bad that it threatened the retailing business.

What was going out of the world was the understanding that it was worthwhile to care about other people. Few people lived in a neighborhood any more. Life was being organized to keep people distant from one another. Human beings were beginning to feel like guests on their own planet. The designers of this building were more interested in glorifying a bunch of oil pirates with an impressive raised plaza than in providing a few trees and benches where people could sit and talk to each other. He turned the radio on again.

"Al?"

"Hold on. He's awake."

"Joe? Are you all right?"

"What is this, 'He's awake,' crap? I've been up here writing letters and rinsing out a few things."

"Fella was spelling me on the monitoring, that's all. Try to stay loose."

"I'm loose, you're the one who sounds tired. Listen, they're going to come up for me—"

"We've been working on that. You're going to get air support."

Leland was silent. If the police could control the roof, they could lower men onto it. They needed Leland to get that close. Support, hell: they wanted him to cover their landing. As far as they were concerned, he was expendable. They had even managed to get a public-relations face on it, calling it "air support." Now the gang had another reason to want him dead. So much time had passed since they had locked him up here that it was possible they had stopped monitoring channel eleven.

"Look, I'm not sure that will work. This roof is covered with structures that will give them damned good cover. They came to stay. It's odds-on that they have rockets."

"Only one way to find out, right, brother?"

Now they were brothers, Leland thought. Hell, he could hear the con in Al's voice! "Look, kid, we can talk about this honestly, but don't bullshit me, please."

"Something I should have told you, Joe. The networks are here, and they're picking up and sending out everything we're saying."

Leland sighed. "Am I getting paid?"

"I don't think so."

"They'll have to take their fucking chances with the rest of us."

121

His voice was controlled. "It's Christmas morning back east, Joe. Little kids are watching."

"They should be in church. Sure—if anybody out there wants to do something for me, he can go to church."

"There you go. Everybody knows you've been through hell—now you've got me doing it. Merry Christmas, everybody! Joe, we're not kidding you. With first light, we'll have helicopters overhead constantly. They're going to cover you."

"Listen to me. Listen carefully and *think!* The only reason I'm still alive is because they know they have the situation under control. They *want* to shoot down a helicopter."

"No, Joe, they want air time. They want to patch into the networks. They want to hook up to the satellite and talk to the whole world."

"And?"

"The people we've been able to talk to so far say that it's difficult, if not impossible, to give them what they want. We're trying to talk to them about it."

And at first light, the helicopters would attempt to get what remained of the SWAT team down. If they succeeded, the men would fight their way down to the hostages, many of whom would be killed. Among the dead, Steffie, Judy, and Mark.

But the police were going to fail. The job would be surrendered to the army, which would blow its way in from above and below. The army would succeed, and then all would die. Leland decided not to argue any more.

"Joe, are you awake enough to talk to a friend?"

"You *sound* like you're on television."

"Go easy on me man. I want to go home and see what Santa left under my tree."

"People keep giving me machine guns." He was moving again, trying not to let the pain show in his voice. "Got six of them so far."

"I thought you said seven."

"Oh, I got seven of *them*. The last was Hannah over there."

"How do you know her name?"

The police had to get a picture of what had happened in

122

here. "I wanted to talk to her about poetry. What's this about a friend?" He saw that he had an interesting dilemma: if he had enough light to see what he was doing, he would not be able to do it for long.

"Well, you have a choice of two, Billy Gibbs or Kathi Logan."

"Tell Billy Gibbs that I'm still flying point. He'll know what I mean."

"Then you want to talk to Miss Logan?"

"*Ms.*"

"Hey, I had to do that in front of the whole country. Billy Gibbs heard you on television and he says to come out of the sun, whatever that means."

"It means that Billy knows who the Captain is, that's what it means." It wasn't bad advice, actually. Leland struggled to the east side of the building.

"Was that your rank during the war?"

"Are you going to let me talk to Kathi or aren't you?"

"I'd better, or I'm going to get bad fan mail."

"I keep forgetting we have an audience. They missed half the show."

"You keep saying that. Are you sure you killed seven?"

"So far."

"And that there were originally twelve?"

"I heard them say that—and not for my benefit, either."

"What do you mean by that?"

"We've been playing cat-and-mouse up here since nine o'clock last night. If any of them live through this, we're going to have a reunion next year. Pizza and bowling. Put Kathi Logan on before your switchboard lights up, hambone."

"Boy, I'm glad I don't ride a black-and-white with you."

"Joe? It's Kathi, Can you hear me?"

"As if I were in the candy store around the corner. Want to go to the movies? How are you?"

"I'd love to go to the movies. I'm fine—how are you? I have the television on and it looks like a war up there."

"Nah, just one dumb cop trying to quiet down the neighborhood."

"They're saying what you've done so far."

123

"You can say it."

"No, I can't."

"I understand. Listen, kid, this is what I was trained for. There's a young lady lying over there who called me a trained dog. These people have a habit of trying to deny your humanity. Do you care who's listening?"

"Besides me, no. I'm interested in who's talking."

"Trained I am; a dog I'm not, or any other animal. I'm a human being, just one, and they can't see that my presence here ought to teach them something."

"I agree with you, Joe, but I don't know if I'm as brave as you are."

He was looking for a way in through the roof. If the five survivors were monitoring him, let them think that he was having a chat with his girl. He could smell her perfume. He could feel her lips on his lips again. Thank God—it was what fate had left him to believe in. "Okay, this is a personal call. Did you listen to your tape?"

"Yes."

"I was cut off by these people. They didn't know that I had stepped away from the party to call you. I got upstairs. I saw them kill a guy named Rivers. Anton Gruber shot him through the heart. I'm an eyewitness. I tried to flash an SOS, but they sent a guy after me. I sent him back with his neck broken. You might as well know who I am, kid. I've been operating on this corner for almost thirty-five years. The police want a record of this. Do you understand what I'm doing?"

"Yes."

"Can I really make this a personal call?" There was no way in through the roof. "I've been thinking of that place on the beach. It's going to be a while before I can walk, but that's all right."

"Why can't you walk?"

"I'll tell you that, too." The only way in that he knew was through the ventilator shaft, but then he would have no way of going up or down. Even if he could really move.

He was beginning to see that it was in his favor if he could convince Little Tony that he was totally disabled. He had to provide covering fire for the helicopters, if for no other reason than to make the gang think that he could still defend

124

himself. What the hell time was it? Almost 5:30. They would start to see light in another fifty minutes.

He kept talking, almost as if reciting in class, counting the bodies out loud. He had decided to take stock of all his assets, including Hannah's empty automatic. He had a pair of kit bags. Skeezix's Czech assault rifle and almost three clips of ammunition, He had bath towels wrapped around his feet, if he needed them. What else? What was left of him?

It was still a long time until dawn, and at odd moments, because of his exhaustion he would sense the black globe, in which the darkness seemed to press up against his eyes. Pilots, sailors, and truckers knew about the globe.

He told Kathi that he didn't know who had signaled him that the police were on their way, but he wanted to think it was some actor in a Jacuzzi with a beautiful woman. She actually did the work, at his instruction. Kathi understood what he was doing. She said she knew the guy, and that he would be glad to lend them his tub. Leland was studying the crap he had.

"I appreciate this, Kathi. I really do."

"I want to see you when this is over. I want you to live."

He thought again of Billy Gibbs's advice. He wondered how much being four hundred feet above the pavement was going to bother him now, in his condition, "I want to live, too. Al, you on the line?"

"I was trying to maintain a discreet distance. What can I do for you besides get the champagne and caviar? Just don't ask me to wear a butler's uniform."

"Too bad, it was just getting interesting. Listen, I'm trying to set myself up for your suicide charge, and I want to get the sun behind me."

"It'll rise about ten degrees left of the highrises downtown. I love you, man. Do you understand? I'm with you."

"Thank you, Al. Billy Gibbs will tell you what kind of a partner I am, Kathi, are you still there?"

"Yes, Joe."

"Well, as a regular viewer, you know that the LAPD will be coming over the hill at sunrise, if not before." He was trying to figure out how much he could carry. No, he had to figure out what he needed. He had to make a plan. He had to assume that Tony was listening, looking for the way Leland was trying to set him up. Well, to hell with that shit; Billy Gibbs's advice remained the best. With the sun behind him, Leland stood a chance.

Billy knew that Leland meant to go on the offensive. That was right. That was goddamned right. He had become the climax of a horror flick only because of these animals. If God was good, he was going to be able to kill them all. This was not the first time he'd had that thought; now he wanted it more than ever.

"Anyway," he said to Kathi Logan, and, he thought, to anyone who happened to be listening, "What I'm going to do is get my back to the sun so these people will have to look into it to find me. We did it in World War II. From that position, I'll be able to cover both the door to the roof and the door out of the elevator tower. Since I saw you last, Kathi, I moved into Klaxon Towers here. I know it more intimately than I've known most people."

"Joe, I want you to live."

"You said that."

He had all the kit bag straps assembled. This time he was going to attach it to his shoulder harness at his end, while he was still wearing it. His legs were worthless. He had to do with what he had. A rat in a trap would chew his foot off if it would set him free.

He threw the harness onto the roof. It wasn't going to work. If he did not face that fact, he would die. He would die if he tried to stay on the roof. But he could not trust his weight to those clips again, especially if they had to take it suddenly, which was going to be the case. He had less than half an hour left.

"Al, are you still there?"

"Right here, Joe."

"Kathi, stay on the line. Al, I want to talk to Vince Crane."

"I'm sorry, you can't."

"Why the hell not?"

"He's not available, Joe. Stay loose, will you?"

It took Leland a moment to realize: Crane was dead. Dwayne Robinson was in charge again, however briefly. He had devised the roof landing—and if Leland happened to get killed in the process, it would be no skin off Robinson's ass.

126

Leland pressed the "Talk" button. "Al, who is the officer presently commanding this operation? I want it on the record."

"Joe, you don't have to help us. You've done enough."

"Let's get the man's name on the record, Al."

"Captain Dwayne T. Robinson. Now, Joe, you've been under tremendous strain."

"Don't kid me. All this time you've been keeping it light, and Vince Crane is dead. Now tell me what the situation is down on the street."

He was moving toward the elevator tower again. His left leg was completely numb—it was his back that was racked with pain now. If there were fire hoses up here, they might be in the same relative positions as the hoses down below. "Are you going to tell me about the situation or aren't you?"

"Mr. Leland?" It was a new voice, very loud and clear.

"Who's talking?"

"Never mind. I have this little base station up in the hills with enough power to blanket Canada. They had it on television. The garage is rigged with explosives."

Leland had an idea. "You want to get in on this?"

"My pleasure."

"Can you hear me well enough?"

"Hell, Im getting you in stereo. If the FCC saw my equipment, why, they'd just about make me eat it."

Leland smiled. "They have their limits."

"Joe, this is Dwayne Robinson. I want you to back off, and I mean now! You've been at this all night, and you've had enough."

"I'm going to do my duty," Leland said.

"Joe, find yourself a place to hole up." It was Al Powell again. "You've done more than your share. Put yourself in our position down here."

"That's exactly what I have in mind."

He had found the hose in a metal chest like the glass cases downstairs, but it was too heavy to carry. He had to unravel it anyway, to get at the coupling that secured the hose to the water outlet. How long was it? Forty feet? He wasn't going to be able to cut it. In fact, he didn't want to cut it. "Kathi?"

"Yes, Joe."

"If this is too much for you, say so."

"They've already told me they're coming down here with cameras. They're on their way."

The hose was stretched across the roof. "Hey, you with the oversized transmitter: what do I call you?"

"Taco Bill. I'd tell you why, but there are kids listening."

Another voice: "Joe, this is Scott Bryan from KXAC On-the-Spot News. We thought you'd like to know that the churches back East are filled—"

The coupling was frozen. He had to hit it with the butt of Skeezix's gun. Now he picked up the radio again. "Uh, Bryan. I'd appreciate it if you stayed the hell off this channel."

"Sorry. We're rooting for you."

"Stay the fuck off!"

It took two more trips to get the whole length of the hose to the edge of the roof. A quarter to six. He wasn't going to make it easy for Little Tony. Leland would still be able to cover both doors if he took another five or ten degrees of arc to the north. It might be enough to pull them out in the open a little more—although Leland really doubted it. They had been too quiet. They had everything figured out.

Leland himself had to figure something else, and for that he had to get up on the metal frame supporting the sign around the building. For the last half hour he had been keeping his thoughts away from this, and now that he had to think about it, he could feel his rage rising. He didn't even know if he could get up on the sign at all, and what he had in mind required at least two ascents. Maybe more.

He pulled himself up with his arms, like a child. Four hundred feet. Smoke was still rising from the street. The officer's body had been removed, but the look was that of a war. The street wasn't what he was interested in, however.

He had to hang his head and shoulders out over the side. The last time he had tried to estimate the distance down, he had been off by six or eight feet. The conditions had been different, but hardly worse. He had to estimate the distance down, the arc he would travel, where that arc would take him, and then translate it all into the length of the hose. If he secured the hose properly, there would be no danger of falling. He might wind up hanging by the waist three hundred and seventy feet above the street, like something in a shooting gallery.

The first moments were critical. Given his condition, he was going to have to roll off the roof. He was going to be spinning. He could only hope that the momentum was going to take him back in toward the building again. And he had to calculate his position on the fortieth floor. Once the action started again, he would be safe there, unless someone figured out what had happened to him. Then he would have to scramble for his life again. Crawl.

He was so frightened he could hardly focus his eyes. He didn't know if he should take that into consideration or not. He got the hose up onto the KLAXON sign, measured it off, then doubted his calculations. He didn't want to do it, but he was going to die if he didn't. Now he realized that he was going to have to keep the hose taut while he was lying on the sign, or rolling off would yield the same effect as being dropped through a trapdoor. He would break his back.

He was going to use the massive brass connector to lock the end of the hose looped around one of the sign supports. Around his waist, he had planned to wrap the other end, secured the same way by the hose nozzle, but he was having second thoughts about that. The force of the fall could drive the nozzle right into his rib cage. And if he actually did get inside the building, he might not be able to get the thing undone before he was pulled out over the street again.

He put on the harness and secured the Browning. He connected the kit bag straps so that they became a webbing of three thicknesses. That still did not solve the problem of quick release. He took off his own belt.

By 6:05, he was in position—*his* position. He had been out to the edge of the sign again to fix the target window clearly in his mind. At this point there was no way to tell how much time he would have once the shooting started. It could be as little as a few seconds, not enough to allow him to get the window open—not an easy shot, from this angle. Presumably there would be more light, but he couldn't even be sure that the police weren't planning to jump the gun and attempt to land before dawn. The noise of the helicopters precluded the element of surprise. For that matter, Leland had to figure that the gang right now was on the other side of the door

129

to the roof, waiting for the first sound of the helicopters.

Which put him in no-man's-land. Beyond the law. Now he *needed* people like Taco Bill. He had been driven here in a limousine, wearing a suit and tie. People would recoil in horror if they saw who they were rooting for. The difference between heroes and villains was only a matter of time anyway.

University kids in Germany had been cheering for these bums for more than a decade. Not that they were completely wrong. The police had tried to sucker Leland into a little thing like laying down his life for a mission he knew to be futile. The police were only quiet now because more talk would point to how little control they had over the situation. They weren't telling Taco Bill to stay off the air, Sovereignty had its limitations, and thank God.

Of course, the best thing that could possibly happen to Dwayne T. Robinson in the next hour was the death of Joseph Leland, eliminating a source of embarrassing questions later. Civilization was full of Dwayne Robinsons, seeing everything that happened to them as opportunities for their own advancement and aggrandizement. They were the spoilers of society as much as all the Little Tonys who had ever lived, with Richard Nixon at the top of the list. Assholes. Because of them, civilization ceased to be even a sometime thing and sank into ambiguity. You didn't know what to believe in anymore, or whether there was anything left.

No, Robinson was really playing hardball. As a cop he knew what was going to happen to every one of the people who had died in this thing. When the forensic lab was finished cutting into you, you looked like a boat burned down to the waterline. That's what they called them, canoes. They peeled the skin off your skull, too—it ripped off like the skin of a tangerine. If Leland died, they'd have him all done and sewn back up again by nightfall.

Now he became aware of automobile horns near and far off. People were coming to see. He wanted to think it was typical Los Angeles, but he knew that that attitude was everywhere now. Leland was in no-man's-land: he hardly understood what he was fighting for. There was still no sign of dawn.

. . . 6:41 A.M., PST . . .

THEY APPEARED ON the periphery of his vision, three winking red lights rising over the hills. A finger-three. Leland wondered what the terrorists knew about the tactics of helicopter support and landing. He had one of the two reserve clips on the sign in front of him, and the radio, volume dialed low, beyond the clip. The second spare clip was in his back pocket. Streaks of mackerel had begun to appear over the skyscrapers. The mountains were in clear view, ready for the next ten thousand years. Leland pulled the radio closer.

"Taco Bill."

"You got him."

"Tell me what you see on television."

"Well, you're a pretty good draw. Thousands of people out there in the streets, back at a distance."

"Nothing else?"

"Everything else is secret. We see the building, which looks like you really smoked it, but nothing has changed there, either, not even a light on or off. I know that because that's all the TV has had to talk about. That, and people going to church back east."

"Joe, we can be of help—"

"Hold on, Al. Bill, you be ready for me."

"Right."

"Joe, we don't want you to do anything. You can stop right now and save yourself."

"If I believed it could be done, I'd take you up on it." The helicopters were still hovering. "I don't think I have any choice. I told you what's going to happen. If I were down there, you'd believe me. You'd take my word for it."

131

He pushed himself backward until the kit bag straps pulled against his ribs. He had to retain the freedom to move. The helicopters started climbing. Maybe they were going to show some caution—but not without creating another problem. If they were going to dive down upon the building in this light, their chances of shooting him were excellent. He realized why the gang had not moved onto the roof: Little Tony and the others had the same field of vision from the floors below, and they could see the helicopters, which were climbing higher still.

He had to watch the doors. It would be fifteen or twenty minutes before he had the sun behind him, and the helicopters were no more than five minutes away—less, if that was the plan.

"Al, they can only come out of the west tower."

"We have you patched to the pilots."

"How are you, Kathi?"

"Looking at myself on television. How are you?"

"Never better."

"Is there any way you can do what the police say?"

"And live? No."

"They've cut away from me now. Look up, to the north."

"I can see. So can everybody else." From the street rose the rumble of an expectant crowd, such as one at a championship fight. Leland thought of Kathi's friend, the welterweight. He wanted to ask her if the guy had gone one fight too long, one round too long.

Leland moved to the edge of the sign. He could see people behind barricades only three blocks away, too close. People were going to be hurt. The police couldn't help that—they had limits. Searchlights were coming on, what he would have done if he had been the officer commanding, trying to get a view of what was going on.

The lights, crowd, cameras all fit together as the way the new world understood anything. People had to see what was going on. It had started with the first Kennedy assassination. If people thought, they would see that they had come to expect television specials like this. It was part of the belief most people had about the unimportance, or insignificance, of the individual. They were used to police like Dwayne

132

Robinson, who expected obedience in the face of his own common sense.

The helicopters were swinging around to the west, the light in the sky strong enough to allow him to see their shapes. Leland pressed the "Talk" button. "Kathi, I don't want you to worry."

"I understand."

He thought she did, that he might have to go off the air for a while. The helicopters were now so high in the west that they were picking up the pink light of the sun, still behind the mountains. The air looked crisp and frosty cool up there at this hour, and Leland almost wished he were with them. Almost. He turned the channel selector to thirty, then back again.

"Bill, count backward from ten and then start jamming channel thirty."

"Channel thirty. Counting now."

Leland turned to channel thirty, cranked up the volume, and threw the radio as far as he could toward the south wall. The first of the helicopters streaked to the south. Now the radio began blaring organ music—Taco Bill had patched channel thirty to the broadcast of a Christmas service. The second and third helicopters followed the first, all three blue and white in the sunshine, what looked like Bell Jet Rangers, with large, articulated searchlights mounted under their snouts.

The radio was twenty feet beyond, from a line drawn from the door to the roof and Leland's position. He wanted that extra moment of distraction, if that was possible. The helicopters were still too far away to be heard, strung out almost a half mile apart.

Briefly, Leland looked over the edge of the roof again, making sure of his calculations. The hose was made of heavy canvas, and he had looped the hose around the brass fittings so that nothing could slip or come loose; but he still could not think about what he was going to do, the act of it, swinging out over the street secured by a rig he had made himself.

He had no choice any more. The police had seen to that, and now a lot of them were going to die. While he swung out

133

four hundred feet above the street. He wanted to think of anything else. The first helicopter began to come around, sinking, dropping its nose. Sunshine flared along the top of the elevator tower, far too high to light the roof itself. Leland hoped his own timing would be more precise.

The second helicopter began its descent, the first still three or four miles from target. Leland could hear the whomping of their engines. He squirmed closer to the edge, where he could hear the crowd in the street starting to yell. He was still hidden from below by the lights of the KLAXON sign. When he rolled over, he would have to hold on to the machine gun and the hose together—if he let go of the hose, the shock of his weight might cause the web of kit straps to slip over his shoulders. He would go straight down. Less than four seconds.

It wasn't going to work!

The sunlight was racing down the elevator tower. Leland dared not look the other way, lest the sun itself momentarily blind him. The door from the stairwell moved. If the gang had been listening to him, they expected him to start shooting at once—unless they figured that everything he had been saying had been some kind of trick. He hoped that they continued to have that much respect for him. He had taken that extra five degrees of arc, with the sun above the mountains behind him, shining into the eyes of his adversaries.

The first helicopter was less than a mile away, and the stairwell door, full of the holes Leland had put in it last night, moved again, as if the people on the other side wanted to test its weight. They were watching the approach of the helicopter through the holes, and from more than an eighth of a mile, those holes were invisible. Leland trained the Czech assault rifle on the door, waist high. He was going to wait until the last possible moment. The organ on the radio stopped and a male voice in a great hall somewhere invited everybody to rise for the Apostles' Creed.

The door came open six inches and a gun barrel protruded, firing in Leland's direction, over his head. Leland fired two short bursts—he had to save his ammunition, in case he couldn't load the other clip. The next burst hit the wall below him, five feet away from his toes.

The elevator tower spewed dust as the first rounds from the helicopter struck it. The helicopter was coming in quickly now, and Leland could see the men inside. He squeezed off another short burst at the door before the helicopter roared overhead; then, as it went by, he leaned over the edge of the roof and took careful aim with the assault rifle toward the window he had marked out in his mind. In the shadow that remained, he could not see what he had done.

The second helicopter was making its run, and this time the door opened wider momentarily as the terrorists returned its fire. As Leland got his own gun around to provide cover, he could see the tube of a missile launcher. More automatic fire was directed at him, but they could not take the time to fix exactly where he was. As long as he was on the roof, they could not set up for a clear shot at the helicopters. But he was going to run out of ammunition or have to change clips or get nailed, and that would be the end of his support.

Rounds from the second helicopter tore aluminum ductwork up from the roof and blasted it out over Wilshire Boulevard. The third helicopter was right behind, lower, shooting out the sign on the south side of the building. The first was just turning into its second pass, flying a much tighter arc, and much more slowly. Leland fired again at the open door.

He counted two of them inside. If the police were coming from below, too, then only one of the gang would be guarding the hostages. That was getting too far ahead. He got off another short burst as the helicopter began its run. The terrorists turned from him, and he leaned over the edge of the roof to empty the clip at the window. It was beginning to turn white, the cracks spreading almost the way foam hisses up a beach.

The terrorist shot at him again, the rounds whanging off the frame of the sign. Leland had to wait until the second helicopter came in before he tried to change clips. More rounds whined over his head. The second helicopter started firing, and Leland lunged for the new clip, throwing the old over the side—a mistake, for he saw it grow small, then disappear into the darkness far below. He wanted to vomit.

There was shooting in the street. Leland fired at the elevator tower. He had to save ammunition. He could not stop thinking about the fall. The hose had no tension at all. In the fighting, he had squirmed the wrong way. Now the door was flung open wide, automatic fire poured up at the helicopter, followed by a great, roaring whoosh and a column of white smoke as thin and stiff as a flagpole. The helicopter exploded in a ball of flame that turned the roof cherry red. One of the terrorists scrambled out onto the roof. Leland fired at him. It was too late; if he could save himself, this was the only way, and he had to do it now.

Wrapping his arms around the rifle, his fingers clawing into the hose, Leland rolled off the roof.

He screamed. He did not want to open his eyes. The slack was taken up almost at once, and he was swinging and spinning downward and then up again. As he opened his eyes there was another explosion, worse than the first, and flames shot out in all directions that seemed like only a few score feet above him.

The spinning carried him away from the building, then back toward it again. He could see the street spinning beneath his feet. The window glass was beginning to break away. He grabbed at the frame with his left hand, bits of glass cutting his palm, but his own motion wrenched him loose again. If he didn't gain a purchase now, he would swing back and forth in an ever-decreasing arc, until he was level with the thirty-ninth floor, five feet out from the building.

He let go of the hose and the assault rifle and lunged backward with his right hand, then his left, so that he was hanging by his hands, facing the street. The rifle teetered on the edge of the floor, directly beneath his feet. To free himself of the hose, he had to pull himself up with one hand and unravel his belt with the other. Even if he could do that cleanly, which he doubted, and was able to drop straight down, if he landed on the assault rifle the wrong way, the result would be the same as stepping on a banana peel.

The weight of the hose was pulling him out into the street, and he wasn't sure he had the strength in either arm to resist it while he worked on the belt. It was as if he were being drawn to his death. He cried—he wailed, out of control, his

136

eyes shut tight again. His left arm shook as he clawed at the belt. He could feel it coming loose, but not fast enough.

His fingernails ripped at the buckle. Paratroopers clawed through their clothing when their chutes didn't open. The hose began to fall away. Leland pushed at it, trying to twist against the thin air to get deeper into the room. He was screaming again, his fear and rage filling him completely, with the heat of an orgasm. His wrist felt like it was breaking, and then he lost his grip.

He landed on his spine on the assault rifle, his hands and forearms pushing back against the window frame as his legs and hips fell out of the window. The breath was knocked out of him; the only consciousness he knew was his terror. He was shrieking at the top of his lungs. His hand landed on the rifle and he almost pushed it out from under him. He rolled onto his belly and crawled into the room, sobbing.

There was somebody on the floor! On his back!

Leland was staring directly into River's dead eyes. Leland's shriek scalded his throat, and his heart stopped. He could feel it, and feel it start again with a massive thump. He fell back, whining, gasping, grabbed the machine gun, and fired into Rivers until the gun was empty.

He looked down into the street, where the SWAT team was running from burning debris still raining down, and bared his teeth. He was alive—he had been saved again. He wasn't a cop, no matter what he thought. He was a victim. A victim. Little Tony and his gang kept trying to kill him, his heart had even stopped, but he was alive. He still had the Browning and the last spare clip for the assault rifle.

He looked around: the gang was still trying to get into the safe. Furniture had been piled in the hall to absorb an explosion. Dizzy, the pain glued onto his back like a shell. Limping and stumbling, Leland made his way into the building one more time.

HE HEADED DOWNSTAIRS. Each step felt like a knife in his back. He didn't know if his numbness meant he was going to lose his left leg or not, but at this point he wasn't sure he even cared. He would worry about his leg later.

Now he had an advantage, and he wondered how he could exploit it. Unless Little Tony could take the time in all this confusion to read the evidence on the fortieth floor in the shattered window and the mutilated corpses, the gang had no reason to believe Leland was alive.

Leland was thinking he was going to let the police, too, believe he was dead. Of course, there might be an advantage in having the gang take a close look at the corpses. Let them think they were dealing with someone who had gone insane. Leland understood what he had done—why he had done it. Never explain, never complain. THIS MAN IS A PRICK. Now it was keeping him alive.

He had been trained for this? Policemen had a view of the world that few others understood. It was the way humanity wanted things arranged. No one wanted to know what life—and death really looked like. Every day this country slaughtered seventy-five thousand head of cattle, a quarter of a million hogs, and a million chickens, but not one person in a hundred actually knew someone with a portion of that blood on his hands. People expected the Lelands of the world to dispatch the Little Tonys as simply as the butchers turned lesser beings into cutlets. But you'd better not demonstrate just how thin the veneer of civilization actually was. If you covered yourself with blood, had the look of death in your eyes, you, too, had to be scourged. He was wise to that. He was still alone. He would be alone until he got out of this building. Leland wanted to live. Like everyone else, he had a right to life, and nothing else mattered.

He heard the elevators humming before the shooting started to fade. With only five left at this point, he could plan his killing so that the opposition was left defenseless at every step along the way. It was the only chance to save the hostages, starting with Stephanie, Mark, and Judy. Ellis had wanted Leland to see that he was doing people favors. Dwayne Robinson was incapable of understanding a really serious situation. The guidance systems that had directed the terrorists' rockets into two helicopters would not have been all that complicated to the kid who had built his father's Christmas television set. How many people had been able to see that highrise office buildings were beyond law enforcement, even after it had been shown that they were beyond fire protection?

Leland kept on going down, trying to remember where he would find equipment to replace what he had lost. If the gang thought he was dead, he might have the chance to kill them all. His head was spinning with it now. More than anything, he wanted to kill every last one of them.

In the northeast corner of the thirty-sixth floor, where he had built the fortress he had never used and where he had caught number five with his head up looking at the plastic explosive, he found a radio, and from the emergency lights near the staircases, he retrieved the explosive itself. The sun had risen clear of the downtown brightness, and the office, or what was left of it, was flooded with warm, pink light. Leland went around to the west side of the building to see what he could take from number four, the girl he had surprised when he had come out of the stairwell. Her kit bag was glued to the puddle of blood in which she lay. She had given him the Kalashnikov; now she surrendered a second radio.

She had some candy, but he didn't think he could stand any more. He was hungry, he thought, as he stood looking down at her shattered body, but he wanted a real breakfast, eggs over easy, and bacon or sausage.

Elevators were humming again. More helicopters were in

the sky than ever but all of them were quite high and far away. Leland stepped back from the window. If the police thought he was dead, they could have their snipers primed to shoot at anything moving above the thirty-second floor. He turned to channel nineteen: a man reciting prayers. Twenty-six had some kid yelling at the top of his lungs. Nine sounded with a steady high-pitched note. On thirty Leland heard the man reciting the prayers.

God only knew what was going out over the channels he couldn't receive.

Leland took a piece of memo paper from one of the desks, wrote a note, folded the note into his wallet, and took the wallet to the window. A fire on one of the rooftops across the street was getting worse. He had to attract attention to himself. A quarter of a mile out, a small helicopter tightened its swing back toward the building. Leland waved the wallet, then tossed it out into the street. The helicopter rose and pounded swiftly overhead. Leland turned for the stairs. A noise erupted from the street, the crowd again, people yelling. Cheers. He understood who they were for, and he was chilled, as if he had made a mistake, and tested his luck.

He went down again, to the thirty-third floor, and worked his way out to an office on the northeast corner. It had a television set. From the hills chugged two large, red and white helicopters, great tanks slung to their bellies. They dropped down, swung to Leland's right, and passed over the fire across the street far below him, dumping a reddish cloud over the entire block. Leland turned on the television set and set the volume low.

The screen showed the fire department helicopters going away—from the angle, the picture was being taken from one of the helicopters far above. The air jangled with microwave transmissions. A reporter appeared, microphone riveted to his chin. He was in the street; behind him were four or five black-and-whites, and occasionally an officer in a bullet-proof jacket sprinted past him. The director cut to the helicopter shot of the smoldering rooftop, while the reporter indicated that the fire wasn't serious. Leland changed the channel.

A night scene, with the words "recorded earlier" in

yellow at the bottom of the screen. A black-and-white came into the picture from the right, seemed to shake as it crossed the center of the screen, then wheeled off crazily and into the light pole. Leland remembered something and turned the volume off. A shot of the muzzle flash of one of the terrorists' automatic weapons. Police running. Now the picture went out of control, spun around, and focused on the building with a cloud of smoke obscuring the upper floors. Daylight again—"Live"—showing the ring of destruction around the middle of the building. Leland had done the job; he had aced the whole building. He turned up the volume.

"—And then, with the sunrise, police helicopters came over the hills to try to protect the desperate, former policeman who, he says, has killed seven of the gang. Although three are known dead, the man observed early last night on the steps to the front entrance, the man shot and then who fell from, the guess is, the thirty-sixth floor, and the woman still visible on the roof—although, I say, although these three are accounted for, the information is that the police discount Leland's estimate of the size of the gang and his body count, as it were, because of the incredible show of strength by the terrorists at dawn, just a few minutes ago."

"I should have taken scalps," Leland said sourly.

"It ought to be said here that this is not a pretty piece of tape, so viewer discretion is advised—"

Tape of the street now: with slightly more light, it was possible to see bullets striking the walls and sidewalks. A long, long shot of empty sky, with a bit of the Klaxon roof coming into view. The helicopters appeared as spots growing larger. It took Leland a moment to get his bearings. He was out of the picture, to the left, and from this distance, his contribution, such as it was, would not even register. One after the other, the police helicopters exploded. None of the cameras was even trained in his direction.

"Now comes word from the police asking all those persons here in the Los Angeles area to stop, repeat, *stop,* jamming the forty Citizens Band channels. You will recall that Leland asked the mysterious Taco Bill to jam one of the channels on which the German language transmission had been heard. While no one knows exactly what did happen to Leland, there is no evidence of his death. He is not in view

141

on the roof. Repeating: the police want the persons jamming—"

Leland changed the channel. A blonde woman in a blue housecoat watching herself on a television screen. Kathi Logan—with her hair down to her shoulders, Leland almost did not recognize her. A microphone appeared at her shoulder.

"Did you see anything?"

She leaned toward the microphone to speak. "No."

"What do you think?"

"He told me not to worry. I think he's alive. I've only known him a short period of time, but he's a very special man."

"He said he was going to do his duty," the reporter said with apparent amusement. Kathi Logan kept watching herself on television.

"Well, he's under tremendous pressure. Normally he doesn't talk like that, but people who know him are aware that he has his own set of rules and he lives by them even when it's very difficult to do so."

"He says he's killed seven people. What are your feelings about that?"

Now she turned. "My feelings are that I hope that God has mercy on their souls, because they'll need it. The man in that building isn't young, and he's alone!"

"If there are television sets in the Klaxon building, he could be watching right now. Anything you'd like to say to him?"

She glared at him. "We just *did* talk!"

"I mean now, on television, when he can see you. If he can."

"Just that I know that he's right and those hoodlums in there are wrong, and most of the people in this country agree with me. We don't want killing—we don't want to be threatened with machine guns or bombs, ever. We have the right to live our lives in peace, all of us, and we ought to say so. I think most people are like me. What you see is all I have in the world."

The reporter put his hand to his ear. "Uh, thank you. Back to the Klaxon building in Los Angeles."

Another reporter was standing next to a young black man

with a badge on his jacket. Al Powell: he looked like a twenty-year-old. Leland smiled. Behind them was a battery of television sets, and Powell was holding a two-way radio. "Thanks, Jim. This is Sergeant Al Powell, pressed into service late last night. You've been actually talking to the man inside, Joseph Leland, haven't you?"

"Yes, but not in the last few minutes." Leland watched Powell's eyes, although it did not seem that Powell was thinking that Leland could be watching him. "We're asking people to stop jamming the CB. The telephones in there are shut down, and CB is his only means of contact with us. This man has been tremendously valuable so far, and we know that if he can continue to help us, he's going to try."

"Now, something came out of one of the windows a little while ago. What was that, a message?"

"No, the wind up there is pretty strong, and with all those broken windows, things are going to come flying out."

"What was the object?"

Al Powell smiled. "Hey, finders, keepers, right? Look at all the terrific television sets I've picked up. Maybe we can work out a deal. Let's see that watch you're wearing."

Leland laughed. The flustered reporter took Powell's cue. "This is your communication center, isn't it?"

"Well, actually it's *yours,* but we've borrowed it, and the studio has been feeding tapes back to us."

"And?"

"We're using them to gather information."

"You've been to the city engineer's office, too, haven't you?"

"Hey, my wife thinks I've been here all night."

The reporter smiled haplessly. "Sorry. What's the next step?"

"You know as much as I do. The people in control of the building said we would hear from them again at ten o'clock. We'll all learn something then."

Leland was sitting up.

"And that was the only communication from the terrorists?"

"That's it. The one line just a few minutes ago. 'You will hear from us at ten o'clock.' "

"There have been no negotiations, then?"

"With the situation as it is, we're going to have to wait."

The reporter announced a commercial break, and Leland turned down the sound. After the station's holiday greetings, there was a shot of an oil-drilling platform belonging to one of Klaxon's competitors. Leland wanted to go to the window to have a look at what was happening, but now he was afraid that one of the helicopters would spot him and let one and all know he was alive. Powell knew. The note Leland had enclosed in his wallet had asked for the jamming to stop, adding, "Let me make first radio contact with you. The helicopter attack was ineffective—no casualties on the other side."

It looked like the police were beginning to respond to him, but Leland wasn't completely sure. Cause and effect weren't always what they seemed. He wanted the CB transmissions stopped, and the police seemed to be going along—but Leland was following another line of thought now, independent of what he had been putting into events. It had to do with the safe, the hostages, and the building. What if Leland had never gotten here? What if he had called Steffie and taken the plane on down to San Diego?

The television screen was zooming in on an actor portraying a gas station attendant holding a can of motor oil next to his cheek in a way people never held anything in real life. With the fade-to-black, Leland turned the sound up again, while he followed his line of thought. The terrorists would have seized the hostages, secured the building, and gone after the safe, exactly as they had done. Given the power of the plastic explosive and the number of detonators he had hidden, they could have wired the entire building. Suppose they got into the safe? Then? It stood to reason that once they had opened the safe, they were finished with the main business of the operation.

The reporter on the street below was reading from notes he had developed earlier when Leland had identified the people who had taken over the building. *Unconfirmed.* Leland thought he would lower the next one down in a basket.

These people thought of themselves as commandos, freedom fighters. Having accomplished their mission, they would withdraw. Leland drummed his fingers on the arm of

144

the chair. The television screen showed the building again, blackened and smoking.

You don't blow up a building while you're still in it.

But you *can* blow it up from a distance with the right kind of transmitter. And if you can threaten to blow it up from a distance, you might be allowed to go on your way.

The gang had enough explosive not just to pulverize Klaxon Oil and the seventy-five people inside it, but everything and everyone for a half mile around. If they left via the roof, up into a helicopter, they would be able to see that their bomb wasn't defused until they were on a jet leaving the airport. Everything was in view here. For all Leland knew, that was the only reason why they had chosen Los Angeles. The police weren't going to be able to get into the building from below, even if they came through the sewers, and the gang knew it.

The police still didn't believe Leland. According to Powell, they wanted him to serve them again. While they waited for ten o'clock, they were looking at engineers' maps and video tapes, and still not ready to accept seven when he said seven, or five when he said five, not six or four or twelve. Kathi Logan understood it. He was alone. He had to solve the problem by himself.

He watched television for another twenty minutes, dialing from one channel to another when the reporters started repeating themselves. One of the networks had footage taken in Germany of some of the gang, including Hannah and Skeezix, whose real name was Werner something. And Karl, the brother of the boy Leland had rolled into the elevator, number one. Karl was a big guy with shoulder-length blond hair: he looked like a drummer in a rock and roll band. Leland didn't see Kathi: maybe the director thought she was too upset to put on the air again. His mind wandered groggily. He felt himself falling asleep and had to jar himself awake. Old man, he thought. That had been his first mistake, thinking he had the internal resources for this. Heroes grow old, not just obsolete.

At last, another realization: there was food everywhere in the building. All his life people had been telling him how smart he was, when he had always seen that his best ideas

145

came to him when he was being shown just how stupid he was. He had gotten away with mistake after mistake all through the night. Taking advantage of Skeezix and Hannah because they were young, an old man keeping himself alive on his experience—it made him feel ugly. The food was in the desks of the secretaries and typists; every twenty-year-old girl in the country would have listed it among her assets from the start. Diet crunchies. Crackers, cookies, envelopes of soup, jars of instant coffee. And hot plates for the water to brew it. He grinned—once again, he had come through. If he could balance on one leg, he would kick himself.

LONG ENOUGH. LET them all think he had crawled off into a corner and died. He was feeling pain again, more than ever. The radio had been silent for almost an hour. No attempt to reach him. All right. Good.

He went up, one step at a time. He had been able to make a cup of coffee that had tasted awful, and then after that he had ducked into a ladies' room to relieve himself and wash his face. All in the dark. He had not wanted to see himself. Afraid. He had seen the mirror before he had found the light switch.

He went up, using the banister as a crutch. He was so dirty, he could feel the crust on his eyelids when he blinked, in his crotch when he moved his legs. If he lived through this, he was going to feel the pain for the rest of his life. No sound from the elevator shafts. He figured he would be better off in the middle, between the fortieth and thirty-second floors. Because they had not found him there yet, he thought the thirty-seventh was the safest of all. His chart said that the north side was offices, the south, some kind of typing pool.

He was trying to stay alert. He kept dialing the radio between nine, which was silent, and nineteen, which occasionally hissed with the static of distant transmissions. He was looking for meaning in the crackle of Marconi's ether. That dated him. Predated him. *Steady*. He could feel blood in the towel on his left foot. It made no difference now. In front of the television set he had tried to think of Kathi Logan, waiting for her to appear on the screen again, but when she had turned to him in his thoughts, she had been Karen. He was that tired. There was going to come a time in human history when people wouldn't have to pay six or a dozen times for the right to stay alive.

He stationed himself at the elevator bank on the thirty-seventh floor. He didn't give a damn how long it took. He could get two, even three of them if he had any luck at all. They had written him off. He loved it. Little Tony, Karl, and the woman Leland had heard reciting the letters and numbers on the radio. That would be the end of it. He wanted to hear that electric whine. When you were in an elevator, you never knew where it was going to stop. Thirty-eighth floor, women's lingerie, kitchenware, and toys; thirty-seventh floor, death.

He wondered if he could find a way of getting down below the normal line of fire, but he couldn't bend his left knee. The only thing he had going for him was the fact that the people in the car wouldn't know it was going to stop. Maybe he would catch them talking about how well they were doing, now that they were rid of him.

He had to wait another twenty minutes before one of the electric motors kicked over. A car was coming up from below. He had to hobble from door to door to decide which of the four on the right side it was. As soon as the doors started opening, he was going to shove the assault rifle in and start firing. He pressed the call button and wiped a gritty hand on his shirt, or what was left of it. He had that going for him, too, his appearance.

The rifle fired three rounds before it jammed. Leland had the Browning out when the doors fully opened—the car was empty. The doors started closing again. He hit the rubber bumper on the edge of the door with the barrel of the Browning. As the doors rolled open a second time, Leland peered inside.

A small trunk on the floor, and in the inside corner next to the control panel, on an aluminum tripod, a television camera. The doors began rolling again. Leland grabbed the camera by the top of the tripod and pulled it out of the elevator onto the thirty-seventh floor. If he had had to give himself away and jam his machine gun for a television camera, he might as well have it. And get moving, too, because the gang would be after him again.

He lugged the thing toward the stairs.

He had to pull the desks out of the way to get to the open window. He stood in the shadow and turned on channel nine.

"Powell, are you there?"

"Hey, Joe, where've you been keeping yourself?"

"I've been around. Look, I want to let you have another souvenir, but I don't want to step out where I can be seen until I know some young genius isn't going to put one in my rib cage."

"Okay. Hold on." The radio went dead. "You're clear. What have you got for us?"

Leland told him. "You said they wanted to go on the air? They had the equipment for television."

"Black and white or color? I'm going into the business."

It made no sense to tell Powell he had seen him on television. "Well, I spoiled their fun. It wasn't what I had in mind, but it'll have to do."

He tossed the television camera out into the bright morning air. As he watched it plunge like an arrow toward the street, Leland asked himself if Little Tony was really so uncontrolled an egomaniac as to put himself on television for no good reason. The answer was no, he had a reason. While he stood in the window, Leland raised the jammed assault rifle over his head. If Tony was watching a television set, he could believe that Leland was still a player in the game. The pilot of the police helicopter pressed his hand against the plastic bubble in a salute. It was time to get out of sight.

He was thinking of Tony . . . and the safe. Given the freedom-fighter pose in the window, Little Tony expected Leland to take the initiative again. In reality, Leland had only the Browning—but enough explosive to turn the Klaxon building into Wilshire Canyon. Tony had to think of the explosive, too. Perhaps he was convinced at last that Leland was liable to do anything. The trick was to keep him off balance. The situation had not changed. In spite of the

149

daylight and the electronic penetration, Leland remained independent. It was to his advantage to let Little Tony think otherwise—that he was the "trained dog" that had beaten and shot Hannah to death. As things now stood, Tony thought Leland was still trying to break down their defenses against the police. Leland set out for the thirty-third floor, where Tony would not be looking for him. It was time to free the hostages, before the ring around them was drawn too tight.

The assault rifle was hopelessly jammed. He needed tools to get into it, and even then there could be a broken part, like a spring. He put it in a desk drawer. He had no need for deadweight, and leaving it where it could be seen was just foolish.

He turned the television set on, the sound very low. One of the elevators was running, and Leland assumed it was a trick to draw him out. He was curious about what they could have arranged. Enough of that—they wanted him curious. At least they didn't believe he could be frightened.

The radio was still silent. On the television screen, the reporter jabbered animatedly, looking up. The director cut to a shot of the building, labeled "live." The camera zoomed up to the window in which Leland had just been standing. What the hell was the use of that? The reporter again. The picture broke up and the building reappeared, labeled "recorded earlier."

It was the same shot, but now Leland could see a blackened, ragged figure holding up the useless gun. On the screen he was not so much nightmarish as pathetic. Like something from a concentration camp. Now the director cut to a helicopter shot, tracking the police helicopter floating in front of it, the building swinging into view beyond. There he was again, recorded earlier, gun aloft. Leland turned the sound off. He wanted to think. Television was another tool, if he could figure out how to make it work. If he could communicate what he wanted without giving the game away.

More than that: without even having heard the announcer's words, Leland knew that he had been telling the world what it had just seen, and was about to see again. Tony had a television set. The people in charge of what went out

150

over the air had revealed his position in a situation that was still life and death.

He wrote another note, strapped it to a staple gun with rubber bands, and put it in his kit bag. The police were able to retrieve notes thrown from the northeast corner. On the way he took a fireax from the wall, to break the window.

What he wanted was complicated, and he hoped that he was being clear. If he saw a television helicopter on station a quarter mile to the east, he would go to the windows of the thirty-fourth floor, where he would put on a show of pushing desks around. The television people would put him on tape, which they would broadcast for the first time at exactly 9:28, calling it "live." He and Powell could add the dialogue then, over the radio. Leland guessed that Little Tony would know within a minute it was another of Leland's tricks, but that was all Leland thought he needed to sweep the glass on the stairs out of the way with the towel on his foot, and get down onto the thirty-second floor.

The window was harder to break with the ax than he had thought, and then it shattered with a noise like an explosion. People half a block away on Wilshire Boulevard started running for cover. He could see broken windows and blackened walls everywhere for blocks around. He chucked out the staple gun and started away, hefting the ax like a woodsman. It was a good idea—it would work. The hostages would be headed down the stairs by 9:45. All Leland had to do was hide out another nine minutes.

The elevator again—more than one. The doors rolled open and someone shouted in German. Leland went down before the firing began, the sounds tearing through the glass partitions. They had seen him on television getting rid of the staple gun! He let go of the ax and crawled across the office floor. More shooting, high and low. They wanted him so badly they didn't care what was seen and heard on the street below. The next office led nowhere but back to the elevators. He drew the Browning and got behind a desk, his back to Wilshire Boulevard. The sound of the firing grew closer. The next burst crossed the top of the desk and brought the ceiling and walls down on top of him. Leland huddled down, trying to protect his head.

The next burst went in another direction. Someone

shouted and there was another burst that sounded even farther away. More window glass shattered. A police helicopter made a run past the building, its engine pounding. He had to get moving, but he was buried by his own weight in debris. He had to crawl out from under it—he had been crawling all night and now again, in the daylight. He picked up the ax. Even with almost all of the glass partitioning down in here, there was nothing to see. The helicopter was gone, and the two terrorists either had retreated to the stairs, or were hidden by the debris still upright. The Browning drawn, Leland made for the stairs. He had to get up one flight for his rendezvous. He still had almost six minutes.

Now he saw in the glass at the other end of the building the reflection of one of the terrorists behind the elevator bank. He was crouching against the wall, waiting for the helicopter to return, and he didn't see Leland. Leland moved faster, trying to get to cover.

The terrorist's radio suddenly erupted with Little Tony's voice, in German. He was speaking much too quickly and excitedly for Leland to understand him. Leland reached the door of the northwest staircase, and the sound disappeared.

He hesitated. Tony had been smart enough to send two of the gang after Leland when the television coverage had given him away. What had been all that on the radio? 9:24— four minutes to go. He wanted to stay concealed until the last moment. The gang still did not know he was without a machine gun—or had Tony figured that out, too?

At 9:26 he opened the door and looked around. Clear. Daylight was no longer his natural habitat. He was beginning to descend the stairs when the door directly below opened.

He couldn't help smiling. He backed out onto the thirty-fourth floor and eased the door closed carefully. If Bozo came out on this floor, Leland would be waiting for him, and if he kept going up, turning his back to the door, that wasn't bad, either.

More than four hours had passed since he'd tagged one of them. For a moment Leland was afraid he was going to find he had lost his taste for killing. He brought the ax over his head. The guy was on the other side of the door, his shoes grinding on the concrete. If Leland had had any sense, he would have fitted himself with somebody's shoes at the start

152

of the evening. You weren't supposed to wear a dead man's shoes. He had been too civilized. The doorknob turned slowly, making Leland doubly wary. Tony had figured something out—suddenly Leland was sure of it.

The door eased open into the stairwell. First the muzzle of Bozo's Kalashnikov—it was the guy Leland had just seen on the thirty-third floor, one of the two who had been trying to kill him. Leland brought the blade of the ax down on his forearm, knocking the gun down and pulling the guy out of the doorway. The ax had gaffed him—he was too stunned to scream. He rolled over on the floor, holding his arm, and Leland hit him again. It was easier than a cleaver going through a chicken. Now the guy couldn't scream. He was still alive, just barely, looking at Leland, helpless, when Leland buried the ax in his head.

"I'm back in business."

He remembered 9:28. He had about a minute, time enough to conceal Bozo, or at least drag him behind a desk and hope that Tony would begin to worry about desertions.

Bozo had a clip and a half left for his weapon. There was nothing else Leland wanted. He headed toward the east side of the building, trying to remember to stay careful. Now he knew what the others didn't: the gang was down to four. This time, Leland wanted to keep the information to himself.

When he turned the corner, the sky to the east was empty. He moved forward to get a better view: there was nothing in that part of the sky all the way to the mountains.

He looked behind him, to the west. Two helicopters, so far off he couldn't tell whose they were. He thought of getting closer to the window, but changed his mind. He turned for the stairs and switched his radio on.

"Powell, where are you?"

"Right here, Joe."

"Not exactly. *I'm* right here."

"We can't go that way, Joe."

"What was wrong with the idea?"

"Put yourself in our position, Joe. We can't yield sworn responsibilities to you, no matter how good a job you've done for us so far. Joe, we want you to withdraw from the battle. You've had enough."

Leland was on the stairs, going down; he was thinking of

153

something else. He pressed the "Talk" button. "Can I talk to Kathi Logan?"

Silence.

"Are you kidding me?" Leland demanded. "I told you how bad the situation was! You wouldn't believe me! Your people are dead because you wouldn't listen to me! You guys are really beautiful—what are you trying to do by this, patch up your image?"

"Now, Joe—"

He was buried by another transmission, clear and booming. "From here it looks like they're really fucking you over, cowboy." It was Taco Bill. "They had it on television. We saw you throw a note down. Boy, you really are some kind of a mess. After all the work you did for them, they don't want to work with you? Well, they sure can kiss my ass. You want to talk to your girl? I'm looking at her right here on television, and I can patch you to her myself, if they have a CB."

"You think you can reach San Diego?" He knew the answer; he was out on the thirty-third floor, moving toward the office with the television set, keeping low.

"Well, that's a kick in the head," said Taco Bill. "She's right here on this screen, and some slicker just handed her a portable CB. Can you hear me, honey? You talk into his microphone, and I'll pick it up off my TV and relay it to your friend."

"Thank you very much." It was Kathi, almost as if she were in the room with Taco Bill.

The whole floor was destroyed, but the television set was still playing, and there was Kathi. He boosted the volume, but not too much.

"Hi, Kathi." *Here we go.* "Bill, boost me up if you can, she looks like she's having trouble hearing me." He was moving away from the set, toward the east side of the building. With all the glass gone, the winter sun flooded the floor with white light. "Can you hear me? You look great."

"Just a minute, Joe."

He was watching her from the next office through the broken glass of the partition. She turned off the two-way radio, then reached forward and turned up the volume of the television set. "The network is picking up and relaying your signal," she said. "I can hear you perfectly."

So can I. He almost giggled as he kept moving away. Tony would be wise to this, but it wasn't Tony Leland was after. Bozo had taken the unlucky staircase. Leland figured Tony had simply turned around the two who had just stopped by the police helicopters—Tony had sensed something. He was that smart. He was like an animal. Maybe he already knew that Bozo was dead.

Leland pressed the "Talk" button. "Kathi, let me know that you understand what happened here."

"I do." He could hear her in both ears, from the television set and his radio. He dialed down the volume of the radio; it wouldn't affect the level of his transmission.

"You see," he said, still backing up, "there's a lot on my mind, and I want to get it said before I don't have any more chances. I don't know what you saw of the last few minutes, but it looks like I've run out of luck."

"Don't talk like that," she said.

He was almost to the east side of the building. Except for the kiss, there had never been anything but the most casual, even plastic interaction between them. Maybe even the kiss. Four or five panes of unbroken glass stood between the television set and him. This was going to take a lot of dead reckoning. He felt another failure of nerve. He pressed the "Talk" button. "Listen—can you hear me? Say so."

"Yes." Now he was beyond the range of the sound of the television set. At least Taco Bill was still patching the signal into the Citizens Band channel. Leland saw that he would be giving himself away if he told Bill to stay with it.

"Pretend we're alone," he said into the radio. "I want to pretend there's nobody listening but you and me. The worst thing in the world is one human being using another." He lowered his voice. "It's an awful way to start a relationship. Do you understand what I mean?"

"Yes."

"Don't just listen, talk. I want to hear your voice." It would give him the chance to move around. He thought he had heard something, a cracking sound like somebody stepping on broken glass.

"I understand what you're doing, Joe," she said. He lowered the volume on the radio a little more, then switched to channel nineteen. It was silent. He wished he could hear the television set. He went back to nine. "It's very important for you to remember that the rest of us out here know and believe that what you're doing, as unhappy as it is, is for us all."

He was supposed to say something. "It weighs on you. They're hardly more than kids." *Now talk—keep talking*. He turned back to nineteen and strained to hear what was happening in the room. Another crunch of glass. Leland was almost on the floor, like a turtle, trying to get closer.

"Nein! Nein!"

Leland could hear it near and far, Little Tony's voice, on two radios; but then, in the next second, as if the act had been too far along to be stopped, a machine gun went off. Leland pulled himself up and poured the full clip through the windows in that direction. As the glass fell like snow off a roof he could see the guy's shadow briefly, spastically dancing in the impact of the rounds hitting him. Before Leland moved forward, he inserted the remaining half clip. He picked up the radio and pushed the "Talk" button, "I'm doing you a favor, Tony. I'm letting you know I'm alive."

"You stupid braggart—"

"Tony, I'm looking forward to killing you."

"That remains to be seen."

"Ah, well, I have other calls to make. It's Christmas, remember?" He turned to channel nine. "Kathi, can you hear me? You'll have to talk into the radio now."

"Yes, yes, I can."

"How about you, Bill?"

"I'm all ears. I'll show you sometime. How are you?"

"Okay. Kathi, I'm sorry, truly sorry. I meant what I said about using people, but I had no choice."

"I knew what you were doing. Now I'm beginning to feel it."

Leland shuddered: he had stretched his luck again. "Credit yourself with a third of an assist, Bill. The other third goes to Billy Gibbs—" He was looking at his ninth victim. He had killed nine young men and women since nine o'clock last night. This one had three in the chest and one in

156

the cheek below the right eye. The face was twisted out of shape, but the blood was still spreading. The guy was alive—Leland felt sick. He took out the Browning and administered the *coup de grace*. Again he had tested his luck—he had a bad feeling about himself, an awful feeling.

"Billy always knew how to keep a guy alive," Leland said into the radio, but absently, as if to himself.

"He says to return to base, Joe." It was Powell. "Why don't you listen to him?"

"You're the one who's talking."

"Do you want to talk to him?"

Maybe Billy didn't know that Steffie was in here. He could say something that would let Tony know who she was. "No, I don't want to talk with him. I'm all right."

"The mayor is here, and the president of the company."

"Tell the mayor I'm not a constituent, but I appreciate his interest. As for the other guy, tell him that my liability insurance doesn't cover acts of insurrection or war."

"Joe, please—"

"Not yet."

"That's right, Mr. Leland, " Little Tony said. "Your daughter wishes to speak to you."

"Daddy!" Steffie urged. "Listen to him!"

"I'M LISTENING," HE said, heading downstairs again, kicking his left leg out in front of him, almost hopping. With three left, whether they knew it or not, they were like a monster with its arms at the top and bottom of the building, and its head on the thirty-second floor. He had to go for the head. This was the last chance for the hostages to get away.

He was so frightened for Steffie that he wanted to cry. She had identified herself. She must have, trying to save her own children. He had only needed two more minutes, less than he would have had if the police had been willing to go along with him on the television scheme earlier. He was at the door to the thirty-second floor. "Come on, you wanted to talk. Let's hear what you have to say."

"Don't bully me, Mr. Leland. I have every intention of talking with you." The transmission was very clear, and it made Leland cautious. "Ah, silent now? I know you're nearby. Does it surprise you that I know that?"

Leland moved back from the door.

"Please, Mr. Leland, you're not going to admit that you're afraid of us at this time. I know you've been through an ordeal, but surely you don't believe you've proved your point. Hannah was more right about you than she realized. You're more than a trained dog. You live in a world of appearances and illusions designed to give your life the semblance of meaning. What do you think you've accomplished with all this?"

Leland stayed silent. He had his hand on the knob of the door.

"You're determined to make a fool of yourself," Little Tony said. "You *don't* know what you've done, do you?

You've been guarding millions of dollars stolen from the destitute people of Chile, protecting the property of the biggest thieves the world has ever known, and trying to keep secret the most disgusting marriage of power and greed. Your daughter? Your daughter knows all about it. You are going to be hard-pressed to prove that you did not know it yourself."

Leland had the door open. The corridor was empty. To his left was Steffie's office; around to his right, the big room in which he had seen the gang herd the hostages. He had to try something.

"You haven't said anything real so far."

"A little more patience."

A strange thing to say, but at least Leland knew that Tony was not within the range of ordinary hearing—which meant, too, that he could be as close as the elevator banks.

Now, from upstairs, a sharp, loud report; the building shook slightly, and from around on the right, he heard people gasp and begin to cry. The gang had not given up; with only three left, they had finally managed to blow the safe. But at the same time, they had confirmed their deployment. Leland grinned and moved around to the right.

The crowd of people looked not nearly as fresh as last night. The men were in their shirt-sleeves, and the women had gotten out of their uncomfortable shoes. They were sitting or lying on the floor, most of them facing the far door. One of the women looked up at him and put her hand to her mouth. He pointed to his badge and then put his finger to his lips.

"Tap your friend on the shoulder," he mouthed, going through the motions. She did, and he beckoned them to stand. The message spread quickly through the room, but not before one woman screamed.

"Get down! Get down!"

Leland pushed his way through the people falling to his left and right. He heard something on the radio. A shadow moved on the wall outside, and Leland fired at it. The Kalashnikov had no more than six rounds left. Tony's shadow withdrew—it had to be Tony, with Stephanie. If he drove Tony back for a moment, the rest of the hostages could get to the stairs the other way.

"Go back!" he yelled. "Go back and go *down* the stairs! Go slowly, there's no one after you!"

Tony poked the muzzle of his machine pistol around the corner and fired a burst, hitting a woman in the stomach. Leland returned the fire, then moved forward. People were running now, screaming.

"Grandpa!"

"Get your brother out of here, Judy!" He couldn't turn around to look at her.

"What about Mommy? He said he was going to kill us all. That's when she stood up."

Tony had threatened everyone because of Leland. "You go ahead. I'll take care of your mother."

"We thought you were one of them at first."

He turned around: now that her face was changing, Judy was beginning to resemble her dead grandmother.

"Go on! Go on!"

Tony stuck the muzzle around again. Leland fired. Tony's burst tore into the ceiling panels. Leland pressed the "Talk" button. "The hostages are free and coming down the stairs. Now you can take the bottom of the building. Do you copy?"

"We copy. How many are left?"

"No more than one downstairs. See you later." Outside, people began cheering. The Kalashnikov had two rounds left. A man was trying to pull the wounded woman out of the line of fire.

"Help me, she's my wife."

"He has my daughter!"

"Look at yourself! You're covered with blood!"

Leland showed his teeth. "Damn little of it is mine."

The man turned away, saying something to himself. Leland looked behind him. Not everyone had got out. There was a man's body in the corner, and near the exit, a second woman was on the floor, holding her leg and writhing. The cheers outside were louder, almost loud enough to obscure the sound of the elevator. Leland spoke into the radio again. "We have wounded on the thirty-second floor."

"How many?"

"Three, maybe more, maybe one dead."

160

"What's happening in there now? What was that explosion?"

"Tony can tell you as well as I can. Talk to him yourself."

"No, Mr. Leland, it's you to whom I will talk." You could hear the crackle of the elevator motor in his transmission. "What have you done here tonight but perpetrate the most bloody, unspeakable crimes?"

"You killed Rivers first, I saw you shoot him in cold blood."

"History will be judge of that, " Tony said.

Leland was moving as he listened, crossing the building to Steffie's office. "Mr. Leland, how many people have you killed tonight?"

"For a little while longer, Tony, that will stay classified."

"You're not ashamed of yourself, are you?"

"Nah." Steffie's office had been ransacked. It took him a while to recognize his jacket, but not because of the mess surrounding it. His pants were no longer the same color. He went into the bathroom.

"The world should know what a savage you are," Tony shouted. "You broke a boy's neck. You threw a man off the roof."

"Listen, you jive-ass son of a bitch!" Taco Bill roared. "Let go of that man's daughter!"

"Stay out of it, Bill," Leland said.

"The man's daughter, as you call her, is an adult largely responsible for seeing that one of the most repressive dictatorships in the world remains armed and in control of millions of helpless peasants. Are you listening, Mr. Leland? What are you doing, Mr. Leland?"

"Taking a couple of aspirins. I have a headache."

He had already done that. He had decided not to try to wash his face again, for he was liable to get something in his eyes. He was coated with grease, soot, and brown, dried blood from the top of his head down to the blackened, encrusted towels on his feet. He could scrape grease and dried blood out of his hair like cream cheese from a slice of bread. He opened the medicine cabinet again, trying to think ahead. Something was nagging him, something added. He took off the harness.

161

"Mr. Leland, for whom do you work?"

I'm self-employed." He was hefting the Browning. The dirtier he was, the better. He had eleven shots. "Look, Tony, you've turned this around on me. Let's do a deal, you and I. A straight trade. You need a hostage. Take me instead of my daughter."

"Of course. You read my mind."

Leland practiced the move for the first time. Terrific—it was going to work. "Now, how do you want to do this?"

He heard gunfire below. That was right: one below, number two was Tony, three was defending the roof. Three left, including a woman. It took Leland a moment to remember how he knew that: the voice on the radio reading the words and numbers. He practiced the move again. Adhesive tape wasn't going to bother him.

"You know where I am, " Tony said. "I want you to take the elevator here, unarmed. When you present yourself, your daughter can enter the elevator, free to do as she wishes."

"Sounds swell."

"Don't go for it, Joe."

"Bill, this has been what I've been working for all night."

"Joe, we're entering the bottom of the building," Al Powell said. "We want you to use your head."

"You tell me when you're inside. In the meantime, I've got to play ball with this guy. What choice do I have?"

"Joe," Bill said, "according to the TV, the cops aren't in the building yet. In fact, somebody's really pouring it on."

"Let me tell him," Al Powell said. "They have fortified positions on the third floor that give them fields of fire to the north and south, which is all they need."

Leland was quiet. Was Tony upstairs with Steffie *alone?* Leland didn't think whoever just blew the safe could get downstairs that quickly. Either way was all right. Tony and Leland were wise to each other. Tony wanted him thinking he was on the fortieth floor. What Leland did not like was the idea that Tony was trying to pull on Leland a stunt Leland had tried—unsuccessfully—on the gang. You get in an elevator, you don't know where it's going to stop next. It was too simple. He picked up the radio.

"Al, you've got seventy-five people coming down the

stairs. You've got to occupy the bottom of the building now."

A helicopter swung in on the building, which rung with the sound of returning heavy automatic fire. There was still one upstairs. He wondered how long it was going to take the police to get wise to the situation down below, one guy running back and forth between two positions.

"I want it known that we still have the weapons to knock the helicopters out of the sky!" Tony screamed. "The people on the staircases will be permitted to descend to street level. We want no further bloodshed. Mr. Leland, are you ready?"

Leland was already climbing the stairs. "What do you want me to do?" One down, one up, and Tony—he couldn't have been able to fire at the helicopter and maintain a hold on Steffie at the same time.

"Get in the elevator."

"I'm starting from my daughter's office, and my feet are cut."

"I understand."

"It's a bad deal, Joe," Bill said.

"I want him to talk. Let him have his say."

"What we were going to do, Mr. Leland, if you had not interfered and caused all this bloodshed, was demonstrate to the world that your daughter and her partners, Rivers and Ellis, were doing what your own government now expressly forbids, that is, selling arms to Chile. One of the mistakes made by the capitalist press is the perpetuation of the idea that we are stupid people. We are not stupid people."

Leland was on the thirty-fourth floor. He thought he could go one more before he had to call an elevator. He didn't give a shit about Rivers or Ellis or their guns. Smart guys. Assholes. Stephanie hadn't even been sure of her bonus. They'd kept her tied in knots. How smart were they now, on their way to the autopsy room? He thought of what he had done to Rivers's body—more bad luck. If you could not wear a dead man's shoes, you could not mutilate his body either. He thought of his daughter again and had to wonder what kind of a human being she had become. He wondered if all this would even make a difference to her, a difference in the way she thought of life.

Tony was on the air again, talking to the world.

"We have been aware for a long time of the secret elements of the contract just concluded between Klaxon Oil and the murderous regime in Chile. Under the terms of the contract made public, for one hundred fifty million dollars, almost all of it borrowed from the United States and its puppet international leading agencies, Klaxon Oil is to build a bridge in Chile. One hundred and fifty million for a single, unimportant bridge in a country where millions live in unimaginable squalor. That itself would be bad enough, but there's more. For the next seven years, Klaxon has promised to supply the Chilean fascist, military regime with millions upon millions in arms. Arms with which to hold their illegal power, power that they seized through well-documented American intervention."

Leland was on the thirty-fifth floor, hailing an elevator. Tony was not so in love with the sound of his own voice that he would not recognize the starts and stops of the elevator for what they were—evidence that Leland was coming after him. What Leland had in his favor was the fact that Tony was on the air. If he tried to punish Stephanie for what Leland was doing, Tony would lose whatever audience sympathy he was trying to develop. He knew it. Leland had no doubt that everything Tony was saying was true. Tony's tragedy was that he didn't see that he was as much a factor—a result—of the problem as the woman he was threatening with a gun.

The elevator arrived; Leland banged the "40" button and shuffled toward the stairs. He would be able to hear what happened. More gunfire from below. Good. Anything to make Tony think the situation was changing. Leland was at the stairs when the elevator stopped again and the shooting began almost at once—and stopped. Leland got on the radio.

"Tony, you're feeling the strain. I tried that trick an hour ago, and it didn't work for me. I'm disappointed with you."

Tony sighed. "Mr. Leland, how do you know that your daughter is not already dead?"

Taco Bill boomed, "You touch that woman, I'll kill you myself, you son of a bitch!"

"That's how I know," Leland said. "Let her go if you want to fight me." He kept climbing: the length of time the

164

elevator had been in motion made him think Tony was on the thirty-eighth floor. It was an open floor plan up there, with the outside windows in view on all sides. *You'd better figure out what you're going to do, kiddo.*

"Mr. Leland, your problem is that you don't know what battle you're fighting, or even what century you're in. Your chivalric notions have no relevance here. You are not Robin Hood and that fool with his radio is not Little John. Your daughter is one of the principals in this illegal transfer of weapons. You seem to know something of the real strength and status of multinational corporations. There are arms stockpiles here in the United States and in warehouses all over the world, where the most lethal weapons are traded on commodities exchanges, as if they were pork bellies or grain futures. We can document the transfers of funds, the money laundering, the attempts to conceal, obscure, and confuse the record. Even as I speak, on your precious, stupid holiday, ships are in international waters, bound for Chile, supposedly carrying farm equipment and machine tools, but in fact laden with automatic weapons, rockets, and other assorted arms. They set sail yesterday morning because the first payment was delivered to this building promptly at nine o'clock, and the signal was given. Six million dollars—six million of the people's money. It has been in the safe here all this time, Mr. Leland. It is our intention to return it to the people. This six million is evidence of Klaxon's disregard for life and human rights in its pursuit of wealth and power. In our redistribution we are going to demonstrate the power of the grip corporations like Klaxon have on all of you. We are going to show how you all dance to their tune."

"Blow it out your ass," Taco Bill said.

"I think he was saying he was going to throw it out the window," Leland said.

"Yes, indeed," Tony said. "At noon, Do you have any objections, Mr. Policeman?"

Leland was thinking of something else, the remark Judy had made about him looking like one of them. Leland was above the thirty-seventh floor, going slowly. He was going to be two weeks in the hospital. All he had to do was live. "Tony, you have an odd sense of social justice. I don't think

165

you'd be as thrilled with the idea of redistributing the wealth if you weren't involved. You'd probably be looking for a secret motive, wondering if somebody was getting a bigger cut than you. That's the way you are—most people listening to you know that already. You made a point before of telling us that you weren't stupid. The most stupid thing people like you do is believe you understand the rest of us. You're not selling revolution, you're just trying to grab a piece of the action for yourself, on your own terms. No sale."

Leland was still thinking of Judy's remark. Tony rarely had been off the thirty-second floor. In the glimpse of him Leland had had moments ago, he had looked reasonably clean, even groomed. Leland looked like one of them? None that he had killed, not Tony, and not the girl who was still alive.

Karl. Karl was the one downstairs. Maybe he had lived through the elevator explosion. He was some tough son of a bitch.

Leland opened the stairwell door slowly. He was on the east side, still believing in Billy Gibbs's advice. He wanted to tell Tony that he hadn't known about Klaxon's—and his daughter's—involvement in the clandestine arms trade. But he knew about the arms trade itself, and everything Tony had said about it was true. Anything that was possible, some human beings were willing to try, apparently including Stephanie. He would be able to explain her behavior when someone was able to explain humanity to him.

Leland got down on his hands and right knee, and pulled himself toward the windows of the east side of the building. The Browning, as big as it was, taped up high between his shoulder blades, gave no sign of coming loose.

Leland and his daughter lived on opposite ends of the continent and saw each other once a year or so. They talked on the telephone every month, when they remembered, or when he was in a hotel room somewhere alone. In Atlanta or Boston, with the day already over in the East, he could call Santa Monica where it was still early evening, and say hello to everybody. He knew Steffie loved him, and knew too, that sometimes she grew tired of him. Whether he wanted to believe it or not, the passage of time had made him old-fashioned. She had not had an easy life, and in some measure he was responsible—but how much responsibility did he bear for an Ellis in her life, or the compromises she had made with herself to get so involved in this?

Leland wasn't thinking about guilt, he was thinking about distance, the distance between people. In spite of his success, money, and privilege, Leland could be in Atlanta or Boston at the end of a day as lonely as a bum sleeping in the park. When people knew who he was, what he had done, and where he had been in the world, they *envied* him—without ever bothering to inquire about his interior life. What was true for him was true for millions of others. Face-to-face, Taco Bill, whoever he really was, probably couldn't sustain a conversation for more than five minutes, unless it was about radios—or drugs, sex, or rock and roll. Over the air, though, why, this was living!

"Mr. Leland," Tony cooed, "I thought you were going to meet with me."

Leland had the volume low. "I'm still on the stairs."

"I know, I know: You're not so talkative."

"I've talked to killers before. You have nothing to teach me."

"There you go again. Rivers was an international criminal. A crime is being committed here, Mr. Policeman—don't I have the obligation of a citizen to try to stop it? Do you claim that what you have done is morally different from, or superior to, trying to alert the world that another of your great multinationals is up to its elbows with human blood? And as for your daughter, what can a trained dog sire but a blood-thirsty bitch?"

Tony meant to kill her, too. Leland was moving along the east side of the building, still even with the elevator banks. He had been sure that Tony would be between them, but if that had been true, by now Leland would have picked up his voice in the room. Leland pressed the "Talk" button.

"You're getting scared, Tony. You were all right when you were in control, but now you're losing your grip." Leland was still moving. "What makes that, do you think? You ought to have more confidence, figuring how right you are. Or maybe it's because I'm so close to you now. You told

167

me to come up here unarmed and then you blast the elevator you thought I was riding in. You're hiding behind my daughter with a machine pistol and you're shaking in your boots. Where's the Walther you shot Rivers with? That's all anybody needs to know about this. You're the one who brought the machine guns into the building. We were unarmed."

"Are you unarmed?"

"That's what you wanted."

"Well, then, stand up, please. I can hear you without the radio. Turn it off."

Leland turned it off before Taco Bill—or anyone else— could protest. He still didn't know Tony's location. It didn't matter—not yet, anyway: Leland wanted to be sure Stephanie was well clear before he went for the Browning.

"I'm standing up!"

"Hands in the air!"

As Leland raised his arms, slowly, making a show of the pain he really felt, Little Tony emerged from behind the desks on the Wilshire Boulevard side. Leland took a step; he wanted Tony to see him dragging his leg. Tony motioned Stephanie to her feet. She reacted when she saw her father, and Tony grabbed her arm.

"I'm all right, honey," Leland called.

"Very noble, Mr. Leland," Tony said. "Over here, please. You look like a corpse already. Come on. What is the matter with your leg?"

Leland didn't answer. He was making a show of it, listing heavily to the right, which tilted his hand a bit closer to his head. Tony and Steffie were eight to ten feet from the windows, with Leland still too far away to be any kind of shot with the thing Tony carried, still too far to be an easy shot with Leland's Browning. He had always been an excellent marksman; there was some psychological theory about it, having to do with one's sense of self. Stephanie was watching him, but not because she expected him to do something. She started to break down. The last time she had seen him, he had looked human.

"I'm sorry I did this to you, Daddy!"

"The avenger," Little Tony snorted. "Implacable. Your father is a man of infinite illusions. He has a pistol in his collar. The policeman tried to make me believe he was unarmed, and now he thinks he is going to be able to save you. He's such a fool. Why should he want to?"

"Out of the way, Steffie!"

"It will give me pleasure to kill both of you," Tony said.

Steffie did not pull away; she threw herself against Tony. It gave Leland the chance to hop forward a few feet more. He wanted her to get clear. This was his job. *Out of the way!"*

He still had the sun behind him. The pistol came out of position just as he'd planned, tape swirling around it. Tony had his eyes on him as he struggled against Steffie. Leland was close enough. He turned and offered his profile, shooting the way he had been taught decades ago, the old-fashioned way, bringing his arm down smoothly, aligned, a piece of machinery. The first shot was the one most pure, unaffected by recoil, and Leland wanted to hit Tony amidships, where the impact would do the most good.

"Kill him, Daddy! Kill him!"

She swung at Tony, hitting him in the face. He was turning the machine pistol toward her when Leland fired, hitting him in the right nipple. He looked at Leland incredulously as Leland's second shot hit him in the shoulder, wrenching him back. Stephanie swung at him again.

"Get clear, baby! I got him and he knows it!"

Tony shot her once in the lower abdomen, not letting go of her wrist. She turned to Leland as Tony tried to aim the machine pistol at him.

"Shoot him! He told me he was going to do this!"

She pushed against Tony again. Leland shot a third time and missed. Eight left. Tony backed up, holding Stephanie. Leland reset himself and started shooting again. The first hit Tony in the stomach, three inches above the navel. Leland squeezed another, driving Tony back against the glass. The third shot was between the other two, and went clean through him, turning the window white. Tony was still clinging to Stephanie, falling backward. Leland fired three more times, not missing, almost cutting him in half.

Tony fell against the window, pushing it out with his back, holding onto Stephanie by her wrist, then hooking her wristwatch with a finger, falling out, pulling her out with him. He was already dead; Leland heard Stephanie scream all the way down.

Outside, people shouted and cheered. Leland screamed, too, holding Stephanie's cry long after it would have disappeared from the earth forever.

AND HE KEPT screaming, staring at the open window, at the brilliant sky beyond. He turned the gun around and looked into the barrel, screaming—if she had done what he had told her to do, she would be alive, unharmed.

She should have trusted him.

She hadn't even listened to him. "Shoot him, Daddy," she had yelled.

"Steffie!"

What did he do now? What was expected of him, the trained dog? The crowd was still shouting, yelling. What did they have on their minds? Did they want more blood—or money?

Were they angry because they thought they weren't going to get the money? He did not want to go to the window. He did not want to see what had happened down below—but just as much, he did not see the necessity for letting anyone know he had survived.

He did not know that he had. He did not know if he cared. He did not know if caring mattered.

He had not moved. He recognized what he was feeling. He had felt it when his mother had died, when his marriage had broken up, and again when Karen had died, the feeling that it was time to quit, that he would be better off dead. It was on him all over again, as if it had never gone really far away after all. Something in us always wanted to die. No forgiveness—never any forgiveness in life. What did it say of a man, if he outlived all the women who had ever loved him? A man like him, with a gun in his hand? What did a gun mean, except death?

He shuffled back to the east side of the building and picked up the radio.

"—inside. Joe, if you can hear me, repeating, we are inside and some of the hostages are beginning to reach us."

He decided to leave the radio on. From the street came a voice calling for the money. What did they use to call those guys at the ballpark? Leather lungs. Six million dollars. For arms. Guns. *Shoot him, Daddy.* Millions for a bridge. Millions upon millions as if there were some use at all to the money madness and the hoarding up of treasure. As if it could add a day to your life. As if you could eat more than two eggs in the morning, Steinbeck once said, which was all you needed to know about the limits of life. What had Stephanie been looking for? What lessons in life had made her believe in it? What had made Little Tony believe in revolution?

Six million dollars. The president of Klaxon was down in the street, looking at the ruin of his corporate headquarters and wondering if his insurer was going to bug out on him. Leland had worked for an insurance company, so he knew it was damned well going to try. Insurrection? Act of war? No, the arms deal itself, which, because it was outside the law, voided Klaxon's coverage. It made Leland smile. How much pain can you inflict on an oil company? How much could it absorb, before the stockholders insisted on people going to jail? He had two rounds left in the Browning, all he needed. *Merry Christmas, everybody.* He started up the stairs again, crying like a child.

In her childhood, he and Steffie played checkers and Monopoly. She'd been born at the start of the war, and he had seen little of her the first four years of her life, one separation lasting almost two years. When he came home, he and Karen tried to make it up to her, sensing that she had been damaged by the war as much as them, but in ways no one could see. They tried to make it up to her. . . .

What you don't know in all your worry and concern is that later in your life the memories that matter most are of ordinary life. Checkers and Monopoly. Their relationship had fallen apart again while he'd been drinking, but when

172

she had come to recognize that he'd stopped for good, it had grown better. He hadn't liked her husband, Gennaro.

She would be alive now if he'd surrendered and functioned as an observer or made his way out of the building to call the police. No, he couldn't be sure. He couldn't remember why he had done so many things through the night. In all, it would have been better for him if he had missed the plane in St. Louis. The accident outside the airport could have stopped him. It would have, if he had surrendered to fate. No, he had pulled a gun to keep to his schedule. He should have paid attention to what something had been trying to tell him. It was as if he had been rushing to see his daughter die.

Any cop would tell you, sooner or later you were aware of every mistake you had ever made. He had made mistakes under pressure all his life. The mistakes were as much a part of human nature as the situations that created them. Maybe Little Tony had had the time to realize what he had done wrong. Tony had known about the gun behind Leland's neck, but had died anyway. It was Steffie who had made it possible for Leland to put one bullet after another into him. She had been sorry for what had happened to her father. She had held herself responsible. No one had thought of that.

Leland didn't know what would have happened if he had gone for a head shot. He might have hit her. If she had gotten clear, Leland would have tried to empty the Browning into Tony. It might have worked. It might have killed Leland in the process, but that would have been better than this.

He pushed out onto the fortieth floor with the Browning still in hand. No need to be cautious. He shuffled past the board room, where the table was piled high with cash, around toward the staircase to the roof. He was thinking now that he had to do this quickly; if the police were in the building, they were coming upstairs—slowly, maybe, carefully, but they were coming. His autonomy in here was almost at an end.

He moved more quietly when he reached the corridor to the staircase. He could hear her in there, thinking she was safe from attack from below. He was reminding himself again that he was a victim, that his daughter would be alive if not for these people, including *this person:* she would have died hours ago, if Leland had caught up with her. He had understood the risk at the start; maybe Steffie had understood it, too, but he did not see how that changed anything.

He had to keep himself going just a bit longer. Maybe they would figure out who had done what in these last few minutes, the real order in which things had happened, but there weren't going to be any witnesses to dispute Leland's version of events. You spend all your life behind one badge or other not knowing if you're a good cop or just lucky, but one thing finally does become clear to you: better than anybody else, you know how to commit a crime. The Torah said that you weren't responsible for what you did while you were a victim of a crime. The argument hadn't worked for Patty Hearst, but it would for him.

Rule one: no witnesses.

He was not going to jail because of some corporate thief's six million. Under the circumstances, what had been good for Little Tony and nine others of his gang—and Stephanie— was going to be good for Klaxon. As much as he could, he was going to inflict pain on these people.

He swung the Browning around into the staircase. "Freeze!"

"Kamarad!"

"Speak English! Hands over your head!"

She was a little girl, plump, with rosy cheeks and green eyes. She looked hardly older than Judy. Judy was even taller. At the top of the stairs with her were more rockets in launching tubes and enough other ordnance to hold the building for a week. If they had had the personnel earlier this morning, the gang could have come out of the building to drive the police back, inflicting heavy casualties and damage along the way.

"Do you have an assault rifle or machine gun up there?"

She looked confused for a moment, then she nodded yes. She looked like somebody's baby-sitter. How old could she be, twenty? Twenty-two?

"I can see you very well," Leland said. "Do you understand me?" His nerves were crawling with self-disgust. "I want you to pick up a weapon by the barrel, and two clips of ammunition with the other. Don't move too quickly."

She did it, looking relieved, he thought. He saw her less well than he had said: the daylight filled the open door behind her. She had that dark red hair, a full, to-the-shoulders head of it, beautiful.

"Come down, one step at a time."

He was trembling. He wanted her to get close enough for him to kill her with a single shot before she realized what he was going to do. He wanted to stop sentimentalizing her; he didn't know who she was, what she had done, or the people she had killed. If she had been up here at dawn, she had killed the men in the helicopters.

And trying to kill him. Another mistake. This was the price of failure. She was at the foot of the stairs, holding a Kalashnikov, looking into his eyes, frightened, trying to smile. She had perfect teeth. He had the pistol low, so she would not believe he was aiming it at her. He shook—quaked: his bladder opened. As he raised the pistol she realized that he had allowed her to live these extra seconds only to carry the gun to him. She started to scream. Leland could see that she had never lived, that she knew she was dying without ever having experienced most of the natural course of life. Leland thought of his dead daughter Steffie and shot this bitch in the forehead above the bridge of her nose.

Nothing on the radio. No shooting down below. There was more than just the six million on the table: documents, correspondence, internal memoranda, some of it bearing Steffie's initials, an "S.G." that looked like a flower. He wasn't going to worry about police problems. He wasn't going to worry about anything. It would be interesting to see if somebody tried to shoot him when the money started flying out over the city. Would the cops automatically assume that he was one of the gang? Or would that just be the story they gave out? The question of who was right and who was wrong was more a matter of point of view than anything else. If you were in a helicopter, you just might pull the trigger because the money was out of reach. You wouldn't even know why you had done it.

He had to get a chair on casters, and even then he would have to make two trips to the open window—past the mutilated Rivers and the kid with the broken neck. Up here, Leland was the only one left alive. Tens, twenties, and fifties as well as hundreds, all banded and initialed by unknown Santiago tellers. After a job like this, if you had any brains, you shot them, too.

Leland was going to have to tear the bands off scores of packets of bills. Rivers and the kid were in rigor mortis now, complete with bright postmortem lividity, like a couple of starched shirts. Smart guys. Stiffs.

Leland's leg was beginning to hurt again. He didn't know if that was a good sign or bad. The first packets seemed to disappear into the haze, so Leland opened five at once before releasing them. From the street came a shout, then cheers and screams. Leland could hear a helicopter approaching. He pulled the chair back out of sight while he opened all of the remaining packets of bills. At the window, the air caught them, carried them upward in a spangled cloud. More screams from below, and horns blowing, as he scurried after the second chairload. Six million—six million *more,* figuring the building.

The helicopter swinging back and forth outside held a guy with a television camera. Leland made sure to stay back out of view. Maybe they would figure out who had thrown the money from the window, but they weren't going to be able to prove it. He opened all of the packets before he wheeled the chair past the bodies, and the money lifted up like the last fireworks on the Fourth of July.

Leland could hear automobile horns from all over the city. He gathered his equipment for the trek downstairs.

On the thirty-ninth floor he loaded the Kalashnikov and stepped out among the computers. He stopped, seeing what he had planned wasn't going to work. He had been about to empty both clips into the equipment. It wouldn't matter. That was part of the new magic that the young understood so well—it wouldn't make any difference. Whatever he destroyed here could be replaced quickly, or the workload distributed elsewhere. The people in the field probably would welcome the challenge.

He threw the gun down. Let the police find his fingerprints. In fact, he'd see if they were good enough to find them. One thing that was *not* going to happen: the police and Klaxon were not going to make him the fall guy.

Not even for his goddamned trick badge. Six million and the building, that was enough damage. Maybe as much as twenty-five million, enough to trigger panic selling on Wall Street. The president of Klaxon Oil, whoever he was, could not yet imagine the trouble Leland was going to bring down upon him. Somehow.

None of it was going to bring Stephanie back. He wanted to know when—how long ago—her life had slipped beyond his reach.

He turned the radio volume up. "This is Leland. I'm coming down."

"Hi, Joe." It was Al Powell. "Where are you?"

He did not want to be caught in a lie. "The thirty-ninth floor, on my way down from the fortieth. I just got the last of them up here. Did you get the one down there?"

"We haven't seen anybody. Now what do you mean, you got the last of them up there?"

"I told you I heard them say there were twelve. I kept very careful count. Since I went off the air after nine o'clock, I killed four more, including Little Tony—"

Taco Bill let out a rebel yell.

"We saw two," Al said. "They landed on a black-and-white."

"No. One of those was Little Tony. The other, whom he killed, is my daughter, Stephanie Leland Gennaro."

"Take it easy, Joe."

"No, I want to get this straight. I killed three others besides him, two men and a woman. The woman is the last—she's on the fortieth. I told you I kept count. I killed eleven—"

"Come on, Joe—"

He was on the thirty-eighth floor. "No, listen to me, damn it! There was one downstairs. If you're not sure you have him, make sure. His name is Karl. I killed his brother and he knows it. He's a tough bastard, covered with dirt and blood. Like me. Find my granddaughter. She'll tell you that one of

177

them was covered with soot and maybe blood. That's the one I didn't kill. Do you understand? I didn't get anyone like that."

"Joe, why don't you sit down and wait until we get to you? If the roof is clear as you say, then we'll be able to put men on it—"

"I have one shot left. The guy has been listening to us right along. How far up into the building are you?"

"There are people coming out of all four staircases. We have only your word that you have as many as you say—or that there were twelve to start. I'm not asking, Joe, I'm telling you: appreciate our position. Let us do our job."

"There's one more," Leland said.

The pain was increasing, but he had fallen into an easy, slow cadence that allowed his arms and shoulders to take his weight on the banisters. He was finished—he was going to get out. He needed medical attention. At the rate they were going, the police wouldn't get to him for hours, even if they came down from the roof. If they tried to lift him to a helicopter, they might just drop him down to the street. Accidents happened. All concerned would be better off if this thing remained a mystery.

He marveled at himself: he was still afraid of falling, even after Steffie had already done it. It made him sick to his stomach. He had one shot left with Karl on the loose and the police afraid to come up into the building. It was as if people wanted him to die. Certainly the president of Klaxon Oil. After this night, the list was longer than ever.

On the way down he tried to figure out everything that had happened and where all the bodies were, but he was too tired, so tired he wasn't sure he was going to be able to remember even after he'd had the rest he needed. He would let other people worry about it. He was going to get to sleep. He wasn't going to think. He would answer questions later. The first person he would talk to was his lawyer.

At the thirty-second floor, he thought of looking again at Steffie's office. If he wanted to live, he would have to forget things like that. After the medical attention, he needed a bath, one given to him, a meal, and a night's rest, in that order. He wanted to see his grandchildren. He wanted to talk to Kathi Logan. The kids had a father, but Leland wasn't sure they wanted to be with him. They weren't that young and Leland wasn't that old. It was a thought and a reason to live.

At the twenty-eighth floor he had to stop to rest. He sat down heavily, stretching his left leg stiffly across the stairs. Both legs ached, his back, his chest, and his arms. Coming down, when he tried to ease the strain from one part of his body, another would begin to give way to pain, and then spasms. He knew he could make it. He would be all right once people could see him, once cameras could pick him up. That was what he wanted. He wanted to get better. He wanted to get healthy, eat a steak and baked potato. He wanted a meal that started with a shrimp cocktail, about eight fresh jumbos.

He got up.

He had to stop again at the twenty-second floor and this time he threw himself back on the stairs to ease the cramps in the muscles all around his rib cage. *Terra incognita:* he kept thinking of the offices and labyrinths outside the stair-cases, the self-important little bastions of clerical territorial-ity—what if he opened the doors and found more computers, more value, more magic beyond his grasp? He kept going, thinking that an old man believes in himself in spite of the changing evidence, in spite of everything.

On the nineteenth floor they started to hail him on the radio again, and he turned them off until he passed what he thought could be a danger zone. He was thinking of where his chair-bomb had hit the elevator. The wreckage he had seen on television opened the possibility that one, more, or all of the staircases were unsafe, exposed, or both. If hostages were hiding in the middle part of the building, he had not seen them. He did not want to see them. He had one bullet left, and he did not want to scramble the wrong person's brains by accident.

The staircase was intact. The blast must have gone straight out the windows. Maybe the building wasn't that badly damaged. He gave up as an unnecessary risk the opportunity to look out on the two floors. Karl had not established that he had an imagination, but how much imagi-

179

nation did it take to stake out the floors about which Leland would be most curious?

At fifteen he rested again. This time he went out onto the floor. Some ceiling panels were down, windows broken, but otherwise it looked like every other office waiting for Monday morning. He sat on a desk, pushed his weight back so that his thighs were supported, then lay back. He had to wipe the grime off the face of his watch in order to read it. Almost noon, if it was accurate.

He thought of staying where he was.

He had to get down to the ground floor. His daughter was dead. Her children were alone. He couldn't stop. You don't stop, ever, no matter what.

He was barely able to get up. His muscles shook so much he felt as if he were being raised by a bumper jack. The sun was so high now that the light pouring through the windows was pearl-colored. Who was going to clean out his daughter's room? He had taken care of both his parents, and perhaps God had spared him Karen, but he did not want to do it for Stephanie. He did not want to intrude on her privacy. Karen would not have wanted it. He was on his feet, moving.

"Bill? Can you let me talk to Kathi?"

"Sure, man. Anything you want."

"Joe? Are you all right?"

"Do you know what happened?"

"Yes. I'm sorry. If I can help you in any way, please let me."

"I got all of them but one. There's one still running around in here."

"The television picked that up. The police say they have no way of being sure, one way or the other. Can you stay where you are? Can you tell the police your location and wait for them to come for you?"

"This fellow's listening to every word we say. He's in here somewhere."

"Joe, he's not your responsibility—"

"She's telling you the truth, Joe," Al Powell said, "Look, I believe you. I don't want anything to happen to you!"

"I'm not looking for him! I'm trying to get out of here!"

"Please, Joe—"

It was like living your life for nothing. What was left? Everything he and Karen had worked for, everything they had planned, and all that had survived the disaster they had made together, was gone. It was just history and the passage of time. He pressed the "Talk" button. "What else is happening? What are they showing on television?"

"The streets of Los Angeles are jammed with cars," Kathi said. "People are trying to follow the money, which is blowing east. The building is between Beverly Hills and the direction the money is taking, and people in their Rolls-Royces can't get around the jam. If you caused all that after what you've been through, if you were the one throwing the money out the window, I'll love you forever."

"I don't know anything about any money. I never saw any money."

"Do you want me to come up there?"

"I'm going to get into the right hospital. Try to get some rest. I want everything to slow down."

"I'll be watching for you," she said.

He had forgotten that television would be downstairs, too. Something made him feel a start of fear—he didn't know what it was. Now Al Powell broke in.

"Joe, let me have a word with you. We have people coming down in twos and threes, reporting that there are people up there too exhausted or frightened to move. We have about forty down here now, but no sign of your grandchildren. On the basis of what you've been saying, Captain Robinson has devised a plan. We're sending teams of officers up all the staircases. These men are heavily armed. As they get to each floor, they're going to say so— radio that information to me. I'll relay it to you. You don't have to give us your location. When the officers are near you, sit down on the stairs and put your hands on your head. We'll get you down, I promise. I promise you, partner."

It took another forty minutes; they were being very cautious. He was on the sixth floor when he heard their voices and the scraping of their shoes. He sat down, put his hands on his head, and announced his presence.

It was as if he had been away—out of contact with people—for years. After they disarmed him and Al told them on the radio they had the right man, two of the officers picked him up and carried him down the stairs. There were six of them altogether, all trying to talk at once. Just as well, for he had nothing to say. He dreaded the talking he was going to have to do. He had lost weight; he could feel it in the ease with which they carried him, then passed him to their fellows.

"How are you doing?"

"Okay. I'm okay."

"You tell us if we bounce you around too much."

"No, you're doing fine."

He could hear the roar of voices from above the second floor, even through the steel door to the lobby. He muttered something, and the officer bearing him on the right said that he might as well get used to it.

"Here he is! Here he is! Get back!"

The door opened on a wall of people, police, cameramen, and reporters, all shouting at him, pushing each other. The light was so bright that he was temporarily blinded. A doctor started cutting at the left leg of his pants. He could see a stretcher at his feet.

"I want to stand a while."

"How do you feel?" a female reporter asked.

"Did you really kill them all?"

"Where's Al Powell?"

"Right here." He was standing back six feet, his hand on the butt of his .38, his eyes searching above the heads of the crowd.

Leland smiled. "You look better on television."

"I'll remember that." He stepped away, not looking at the short, dark-haired white man on his left. "This is Captain Dwayne Robinson."

"We're going to have to ask you a few questions, Leland. We're studying the video tapes now, and we're very interested in who got rid of that money, and why."

Leland saw Powell shake his head: the tapes showed nothing.

"I'm not answering any questions without the advice of a lawyer," Leland said. "I think his first advice would be that I get medical attention."

"Let us talk to him," a dark-haired, moustached reporter said.

Leland recognized what was happening with the first sound, to his left, at the door to the northeast staircase. He wanted to get to the floor, but Robinson was blocking him, pushing him back against the wall. Karl shouted and opened fire on the reporters, whose screams and shrieks as they fell almost obscured the sound of the Kalashnikov. It was like looking in the mirror. Karl was covered with dirt and blood. He wanted to kill them all. It was another kind of madness, like the greed that had brought this down on them. Karl was not going to be satisfied until somebody stopped him. Not even Stephanie had been able to stop Leland. Not even Stephanie's death.

Now Karl found Leland. It was exactly like looking in the mirror. Karl could see no one but Leland; Leland knew it. Robinson had his gun out, but he never got off a round. Karl shot first, as Al Powell grabbed Robinson's shoulder and pulled him into Karl's line of fire. There was a ferocity to Powell's expression that Leland would not have imagined from what he had just seen upstairs on television. Robinson backed and fell against Leland, who felt himself being hit again, in the thigh, high up. Before the shock and the weight of Robinson's body knocked him down, Leland saw Powell take careful aim and, with two clean shots, tear off the top of Karl's head in a sheet of brains and blood.

Leland tried to pull himself out from under Robinson. With two hands, Powell rolled Robinson's body away. He tore at the leg of Leland's trousers. The blood felt as if someone had poured a bowl of soup in his lap.

"Medic! Medic!"

The doctor was lying dead beside Leland and Robinson. People were just stirring from where they had thrown themselves around the lobby. People started shouting.

"Give me that fucking belt," Powell said, pulling it loose. "You're not going to die on me, not now." He lashed the belt tightly around Leland's thigh. "I liked the way you ducked behind Robinson."

Leland stared.

"He died a hero," Powell said. "Don't you forget it."

"I wish you hadn't done anything."

Powell looked at him. "I know. But nobody should think that about himself—especially not the guy I'm counting on as my partner."

"Robinson made a mistake," Leland said aloud, but to himself.

"He gave his life for you," Powell said. "That's the only way to look at it. You're not bleeding anymore. You're going to live."

"You're a hell of a good cop," Leland said.

"Next to you, I'm no kind of a cop at all." Now he was crying. Cops crowded over him, craning for a look. A bottle of plasma was being set up. A new face appeared.

"Don't let go of that belt, kid."

"Sergeant," Powell said.

"Sergeant, I'm sorry. That's exactly right. Don't let go."

"You take it easy," Powell said to Leland. "You have years of living ahead of you."

Leland had no answer. He wanted to say something, but found himself suddenly unwilling to think. He realized he could let everything go—he could let himself drift. He felt the whole long life he had already lived recede deeper into his memory. He was being picked up, rolled quickly toward the door. Somebody was holding the plasma, running alongside him with Powell. Powell smiled, the same man who had just looked so ferocious.

Leland closed his eyes. Now, and for a little while longer, he was going to think of flying.

From Ballantine